TALES FROM CABIN 23
THE BOO HAG FLEX

TALES FROM CABIN 23
THE BOO HAG FLEX

BY
JUSTINA IRELAND

SERIES CREATED BY
JUSTINA IRELAND & HANNA ALKAF

Balzer + Bray
An Imprint of HarperCollinsPublishers

Balzer + Bray is an imprint of HarperCollins Publishers.

Tales from Cabin 23: The Boo Hag Flex
Text copyright © 2024 by Justina Ireland
Illustrations copyright © 2024 by Gabriel Infante
Stock illustrations: trees: Jurik Peter/Shutterstock; border:
Perfect_kebab/Shutterstock; ink splotch: Milano M/Shutterstock

Library of Congress Control Number: 2023943345

ISBN 978-0-06-328782-2

Typography by Corina Lupp

24 25 26 27 28 LBC 5 4 3 2 1

FIRST EDITION

For all my fellow scaredy cats.
Meow.

AT CAMP APPLE HILL FARM THERE IS A STORY:

For a few campers a mysterious fog will appear, summoning them to a witch's cabin where they must endure a terrifying tale . . . or else! Why the cabin appears is not truly known, although many theories abound. The cabin does not exist on any map, and while many campers have gone looking for this mysterious cabin, few have found it, but those who have tell of a terror that defies explanation.

ARE YOU BRAVE ENOUGH TO VISIT CABIN 23?

PROLOGUE

Summer camp was supposed to be fun.

It was not.

Elaina lay on her bunk in Cabin 16 and tried not to cry. Two hours she'd been at Camp Apple Hill Farm and she wanted to go home. She hated the food, hated her bunkmate, and hated every single tree and camp counselor.

She didn't belong there. She belonged back home in Maryland.

"Elaina! Are you coming with us?" yelled her bunkmate, a girl named Tiffany, from near the door to the cabin. The other girls had already gone on ahead. But Elaina didn't want to go to tonight's campfire gathering. She just wanted to be left alone.

Tiffany was not good at taking a hint, though. She was *a lot*, as Elaina's older sister might have said. Tiffany had brown hair and pale skin with an explosion of freckles across her nose and she yelled everything all the time. "If I get too loud, you can let me know and I'll try to be quiet," Tiffany had said earlier that day. So far, Elaina found it easier to ignore the girl than to constantly remind her that she was yelling.

"I think Elaina may need an evening to recenter herself," said their cabin counselor, Missy. She had dark brown skin and box braids just like Elaina, and seemed to be able to sense her moods better than anyone else. "She can stay here with Taylor if she isn't feeling up to singing songs around the campfire."

Missy was nice and Elaina wanted to like her, but when she'd told Missy she wanted to go home, Missy had given her a kind smile and said, "Give it some time. You might end up having fun." That seemed to be the end of the conversation.

Elaina couldn't see how she was going to survive another two hours, let alone the remainder of the two-week session her mom had signed her up for. All because her mom wanted her to try to make new friends. It wasn't her fault her best friend, Madison, had moved away right after Easter and Elaina didn't have anyone else to hang out with. She wasn't lonely, like her mom thought. She just really, really missed her best friend. And no one else she knew—no one at Camp Apple Hill Farm, for sure—was even half as cool as Madison.

"All right, who's ready for s'mores and too many verses of 'The Wheels on the Bus'?" asked Taylor, their other counselor, as she entered the cabin. Her long dark hair had been braided with daisies, and her tan skin shone with a sheen of sweat from walking the other campers in the cabin to the jamboree.

"Elaina isn't really feeling up to s'mores," Missy said to Taylor, the two older girls exchanging a weighted glance.

"No worries. You and Tiffany go ahead. Elaina and I can hang out here and get to know each other," Taylor said with a shrug.

Missy nodded. As Tiffany followed her out, she gave Elaina one last forlorn glance.

"So . . . Do you want to play a board game or something?" Taylor asked, standing next to the bunk.

Elaina shook her head and lay back down. What she wanted was to go home. But apparently that wasn't an option.

Taylor opened her mouth to speak, but whatever she was about to say was cut off by a knock at the door.

3

"Yes?" Taylor said, moving toward the door. Elaina rolled over on her bunk, facing the wall and ignoring both Taylor and whoever was at the door. Unless it was a ride home, she wasn't interested.

Whoever it was, though, Elaina couldn't tell. She couldn't hear what Taylor was saying to them.

In fact, Elaina couldn't hear anything at all.

Elaina rolled over, looking toward the door, and saw . . . no one.

She sat up on her bed. Elaina was still in the cabin where she'd been a few moments before, but now everything looked strange. The setting sun was gone; the light coming in the windows was odd, like it was the middle of the night and the moon was shining brightly. The door was open, and a chill, damp fog was drifting in across the threshold. Her counselor was nowhere to be found.

Elaina scrambled off the bunk and wrapped her arms around her middle. "Taylor?" she called, slipping on her shoes and walking toward the door. Her footsteps echoed loudly in the cabin, and when she walked out onto the porch, a heavy fog had blanketed everything, the world quiet. There were no night sounds, not a single cricket or owl hoot, and the trees pressed in much more closely than they had just moments before.

Elaina walked down the porch, and as her feet sank into the ankle-high grass, there was a sound from behind her, the cabin door slamming. She whirled around.

The cabin was gone.

"Hello?" Elaina called, fear seizing her middle and sending sudden tears to her eyes. She pinched her arm to make sure she wasn't dreaming, like people sometimes did on TV shows. The pain was sharp and real. Whatever was going on, she hadn't fallen asleep.

"Taylor? This isn't funny," she called, walking forward into the trees. As she moved carefully through the woods, she turned slowly, taking in her surroundings. A few hesitant steps, and the fog cleared a bit to reveal then that she wasn't in the middle of the woods, exactly. Rather, she stood in a small clearing. She took another step forward and the mist cleared farther ahead of her so that she could see a dusty path. And at the end of the path was a cabin.

It looked much older than the other cabins at camp. The roof sagged, with shingles missing here and there, and the porch lacked a number of boards. And standing a few feet in front of the cabin was a crooked sign: CABIN 23.

Cabin 23? But there were only twenty cabins at camp.

This was creepy—*too* creepy. Elaina tried to turn back the way she'd come. But the fog didn't like that, as it suddenly grew thicker. It turned Elaina around, reaching out clammy, misting fingers that pushed her toward the dilapidated cabin, insistent.

The door to the cabin was open now, a warm golden glow coming from inside. It was the only light Elaina could see in any direction. The fog shoved her once again and even pinched the back of her arm, making Elaina yelp in pain. Fear drove her footsteps then, and she ran for the door, even as a small voice in the back of her mind insisted that it was a bad idea.

Elaina entered the cabin, and the door slammed behind her without her even touching it. Her heart pounded, and a sour taste was in her mouth. She wanted to cry, she wanted to run. What was even happening? One moment she'd been in her cabin, lonely and miserable, now she was . . .

Standing before a woman who looked curiously like a witch.

The elderly Black woman sat in a rocking chair, a small, fluffy dog asleep in her lap. The woman wore a camp T-shirt and khaki shorts, like the counselors did, but Elaina didn't think she could be a camp counselor. There was something strange about the cabin, and Elaina had an uneasy feeling as she looked around the room, which was dusty and had the musty scent of disuse.

The woman eyed Elaina, a blank expression on her face. "You're lost," she said, and her voice echoed eerily. She lifted her nose and sniffed, and at that, her mouth twisted into a smile. "So much terror in you."

"I—my cabin, it disappeared. And there was this fog . . ."

The old woman smacked her lips like she'd just had a tasty treat, and Elaina swallowed dryly.

"Sit." It was a command, not an invitation, and a chair appeared behind Elaina, knocking into her knees painfully and forcing her to sit down.

"If you have found yourself here," the old woman continued, "then you need a story."

What was even happening? No, Elaina did not need a story, she needed to find a way back to her cabin. "What if I don't want to hear a story?"

The witch licked her lips and bared her teeth again. They were yellow and crooked, and the look made Elaina stiffen in fear. "If you will not listen to a story, then you can brave the fog. And I do believe it is quite *vicious* tonight. Hungry. Hungrier, even, than I."

The front door flew open, and that same cold,

creeping fog reached ghostly fingers into the cabin, as though grasping for Elaina. She remembered the pain on the back of her arm, and she leaned back into the chair, avoiding the grasping hands as they reached for her. "No! No, I'll listen."

The fog immediately retreated, slithering backward. It slowly seeped back outside, reluctantly, and the door shut with an echoless bang.

"Ah," the witch said, the front door slamming shut once more. "A story it is, then. A tantalizing treat for the homesick and bereft. I call this one *The Boo Hag Flex*."

Moving is never fun.

Tasha learned that when she was a little kid. Now, at twelve, she was much too familiar with it. No matter whether she was coming or going, if the day was sunny or rainy, moving was always the *worst*.

First, there was the packing: putting everything in boxes or suitcases or, even worse, black plastic trash bags. Then, there was all the lifting, which, when you had as many books as Tasha's mom had, meant you were risking back injury. And the goodbyes: friends crying, enemies smirking, favorite people and places left behind forever. That ice cream place in the strip mall that had the best strawberry blast milkshakes? Well, kiss it goodbye, because you're never going to see it again. And finally, there was never, ever enough time; it didn't matter how many times you double- and triple-checked your apartment, something was always left behind.

This time, it was Tasha's favorite notebook.

"Don't worry," John said as he guided his old Honda Civic down the freeway off-ramp. "I can get you another notebook."

Tasha said nothing and just stared out the window. What was there to say? He wouldn't understand that it wasn't the notebook that was important, even though she had been working all year on the decoration, covering it with the perfect collection of sparkly stickers.

It was that the notebook was the last thing Mom had given her before she'd died.

In fact, Tasha was learning that John, who was her dad and who she'd just met, didn't understand a lot of things. For instance, the fact that just because they shared the same warm brown skin and thick eyebrows, it didn't mean that Tasha wanted to call him Dad. After all, he hadn't even cared she existed until her mom had gotten sick and, knowing that she was going to die, decided to call him for the first time that Tasha could remember.

Since Mom had gotten sick, Tasha had been staying with Mrs. Flanagan, their neighbor in the apartment complex. So it was John and a nervous-looking white woman from the county social workers' office who had delivered the news two days ago that Tasha's mom had died in the hospital, a virus taking her life while Tasha was watching dance videos on the internet. The doctors had done all they could, he told her, looking like he wanted to be anywhere else but Mrs. Flanagan's living room. It was the one thing Tasha felt like they might have in common: she would've rather been anywhere but that shabby, cat-hair-filled living room as well.

"So, if you're my dad, where have you been all my life?" she had said. It seemed like a perfectly fair thing to ask. Tasha wasn't a baby; she knew people got together and then broke up. Lots of kids she knew had parents who were divorced, or who never got married in the first place. But most of them knew who their parents were. They spent weekends and summer vacations with them, had pictures that they put on family trees for school projects. Tasha hadn't had any of that. She had never even known John's name until the social worker had introduced him.

John had laughed awkwardly and changed the subject, neither he nor the social worker bothering to answer her question. Tasha, in fact, had a lot of questions, but she didn't get any real answers to those either, just apologies and mumbled phrases like "being an adult is complicated" and "you'll understand when you're older." But Tasha didn't think either of those things were true and had decided when she woke up this morning in the cheap hotel room John had gotten while they'd waited for Mom's ashes that it was better to pretend it didn't matter. It was better than being continually disappointed by the only parent she had left.

Now, in the car beside him, Tasha took a deep breath. She'd been taking a lot of deep breaths over the past few weeks. It had been Mom's favorite advice. "When you get overwhelmed or upset, just take a moment and take a few deep breaths. There are very few things that can't wait long enough for that, at least."

And all Tasha had was time while they drove, mostly in silence, across the state, to where John lived with his mother. The Shady Pines Estates in Hinesville, Georgia, had sounded nice until John showed her pictures of where she would be living.

It was a trailer park.

Tasha had lived in lots of different places, but for the last few years, those places had mostly been in and around Atlanta, where there were lots of Black people. Did Black folks even live in trailer parks? John and his mom did, Tasha supposed, but were there others? A trailer park sounded like a place you'd meet the kind of people who attended angry political rallies and made racist comments that they pretended were just funny jokes. They'd lived next to a neighbor like that once—not Mrs. Flanagan but an old man with a tiny Chihuahua who used to laugh as the little dog chased the kids in the neighborhood. Everyone had been glad when that mean old man had died, animal control taking his evil little dog. Hopefully it hadn't ended up in a family with kids.

Would Shady Pines be full of old men like that? The only thing Tasha knew about Hinesville was that there was a big army base there, where her dad had grown up. It didn't seem like anyplace she wanted to be, but Tasha knew that, with her mom gone, there wasn't probably anyone left who cared what she thought, especially when it came to moving.

She took another deep breath while John said something about Savannah, that it was his favorite place in Georgia and that they could maybe take a trip there later this summer. Tasha didn't answer. She was only half-certain he was talking to her and not himself. He did that a lot, and over the past few days

Tasha had learned to just let his half of the conversation wash over her, because answering only made things more awkward.

The freeway off-ramp gave way to rural roads, squat houses, and a number of Confederate and American flags. People really seemed to love their flags here. One house had a flag proclaiming "Spring Has Sprung!" even though it was the end of June.

Tasha sank into her seat a little more. Her mom was dead and she was moving to a completely different world. It was enough to give anyone an upset stomach, but she just felt kind of numb. John glanced over and patted her leg awkwardly. His dark face was kind, but Tasha was still somewhat intimidated by him. His head was completely bald, and he was so tall and broad that he had to fold himself into the car like an accordion. He also smiled too much, and Tasha had the feeling that he was mostly saying the things he thought she wanted to hear, not what he actually thought. Mom had always told Tasha that she got her height from her dad; Tasha thought it was just a thing a person said, but now she could see it was probably true. Mom had been small and light-skinned, and Tasha was much darker than she had been. She had also rarely smiled and had only spoken when there was something to say, and usually opted for impromptu hugs and whispered I-love-yous. Tasha really, really wanted one of those hugs now.

She gave herself a little mental shake. There would be no more hugs from her mom. That was part of the past now.

"We can head by the Walmart if you'd like," John said, each word careful, like Tasha was some delicate flower and saying the wrong thing might break her. "Before we get to the house. I'm really sorry about the notebook."

Tasha shook her head. "It's okay," she said. "I don't need one right now."

"Are you hungry?" he asked. "We could stop somewhere . . ." He watched her, but what he was looking for, Tasha had no idea. She just wanted to be left alone, trying her best not to think about Mom. John hadn't even mentioned her once since that first day, and for some reason that just made Tasha refuse to give in to the sadness that loomed on the horizon or think about what she'd lost. Had John ever loved Mom? The longer Tasha spent with him, the more questions she had.

Tasha realized John was still waiting for her to answer, and she shook her head. "No, I'm not hungry."

She hadn't been hungry since the man at the funeral home had handed her the urn with her mother's ashes.

The urn was now in the trunk with the rest of her belongings. Luckily, *that* had not been lost in the move.

They fell into silence and the miles sped by. Eventually, Tasha fell asleep, and when she awoke, it was to the crunch of gravel under tires as they were pulling into the trailer park. A faded white-and-green sign greeted them; "Shady Pines Estates, A Mobile Village," it read. The sign looked old, and as John continued down the gravel road that ran through the park, everything had the same worn-down look. The trailers were as tired as the old people who sat on the porches. As they passed, the old people followed their car with suspicious gazes.

"I know it doesn't look like much," John said. "But everyone here is nice. You'll like it."

Tasha narrowed her eyes at John. Even he didn't sound like he believed that.

They pulled up to a blue-and-white trailer with marigolds planted all around. A large, elderly Black woman with a pouf of white hair waved at them.

"That's your grandmother. My mom," John said. "Uh, you can call her Ms. Washington if you aren't comfortable calling her Grandma."

For the hundredth time that week, Tasha felt hot tears welling up, unbidden. She nodded and blinked fast so that she wouldn't start crying. She would cry later when no one else could see. She hated how the grief sometimes snuck up on her, reminding her that nothing would ever be the same again. Tasha just wanted to get back to a normal life. Whatever that was.

Tasha climbed out of the car, pulling her backpack with her. Inside was her favorite stuffed animal—an elephant named Buzzy—plus a couple of graphic novels her mom had bought her that she'd read to pieces. The rest of her stuff was in the trunk, in the suitcases John had bought for her. She stood awkwardly by the car while he went to get them.

The old woman on the porch waved again and smiled warmly. "Leave all that for your daddy and you come on in. I made cookies. I hope you like double chocolate chip."

They were Tasha's favorite, but she was still hesitant as she climbed the stairs to the front porch. The old woman seemed a little too happy to see Tasha, and she was half afraid Ms. Washington would try to hug her, but the old woman just patted her shoulder, as though she could sense Tasha's discomfort, and invited her inside.

Cool air greeted them, and the trailer smelled of good things. The place was even smaller than she'd been expecting, only as wide as a single room. It didn't look like an apartment or a house, but it was cozy, with everything close at hand. Tasha's attention was immediately drawn to the bookshelves that lined the living room.

"Oh, you looking at my library?" said Ms. Washington. "It's nothing compared to the one in town, but we do all right. Feel free to read whatever you'd like. I'll get those cookies."

Tasha didn't have to be told twice. She made her way to the bookshelves, expecting to find romances like her mom had liked, but the titles on the spines were strange—things like *Cursed Objects of North America* and *Hex Work: Breaking Everyday Curses*. And Tasha's eyes were drawn to one book in particular:

A Guide to Southern Myths and Legends

The volume was heavy and old, like something that you'd find in a museum. Tasha pulled it off the shelf and began flipping through the pages.

"Oh, that's a fun little bit of local history," Ms. Washington said, stepping into the living room with a plate in hand. The floor had an echoing, hollow sound to it that seemed odd to Tasha, but her grandmother didn't seem to notice, so she chalked it up to just being part of living in a trailer. "Do you like to read?"

"Yeah," Tasha said. "A lot."

Ms. Washington nodded. "Your daddy did as well when he was younger. But now . . ." Ms. Washington shrugged and set the plate of cookies on the table next to the couch. "Go ahead, try one. They were your momma's favorite, you know."

That made Tasha perk up. "You knew my mom?"

"Of course I did. She lived here with me while she was pregnant with you. She even sent me pictures of you every once in a while, especially when you were little. We talked about getting together, me heading up to Atlanta to visit when you all got settled or maybe you and her coming down here sometime. But, well . . ." Ms. Washington trailed off, her expression far away. "I suppose you always think there's more time, until there isn't."

The silence drew out into something awkward, until Ms. Washington gave her head a little shake. "Why don't I show you to your room?"

Tasha glanced toward the front door. "I have to grab my bags."

The door opened then and John entered, carrying all of Tasha's suitcases in his arms. He dumped them in the living room before heaving a sigh.

"You both good?" he asked, then nodded before either of them had said anything. "The game is on, and I promised Jake I'd meet him at the Goal Line."

"What's the Goal Line?" Tasha asked.

"A sports bar," Ms. Washington said. Her face changed slightly into something like a frown. "Tasha just got here. You don't want to help her get settled in?"

"It's the finals, Ma. Game six. Besides, Tasha and I have spent plenty of time together. I'm sure she wants to spend some time on her own."

He looked at her expectantly. He wasn't wrong, Tasha thought, but the way he said it made her feel something she couldn't name. Like he wanted to get away from *her* more than she wanted a break from him.

"We'll hang out on Saturday," he said. "I promise."

Ms. Washington didn't say anything else, and John took that as an answer, giving her a peck on the cheek before leaving, the suitcases still scattered haphazardly in the middle of the floor.

"Well, I suppose we should get these to your bedroom," Ms. Washington said with a long sigh.

Tasha gave the plate of cookies a forlorn glance before grabbing the biggest suitcase and following Ms. Washington to the back of the trailer. They walked through the kitchen and past the bathroom before reaching a narrow door that led to a small room. Inside was a twin bed and a dresser, but nothing else.

"We'll have to go to the Walmart and get you some things to decorate," Ms. Washington said, stepping aside so Tasha could haul the suitcase inside. "I got you some clothes since I didn't know what you had, they're in the drawers. If you don't like them, we can take them back to the store."

"Where does John sleep?" Tasha asked. The trailer seemed too small to have more than two bedrooms.

"He's got a girlfriend in town that he stays with most of the time. Her name is Kim. She's a seamstress, works in the same building where your daddy has been doing construction for the last six months. When he's here, though, he'll sleep on the couch in the living room. I hope that's okay."

"It's fine," Tasha said. *I won't cry*, she thought again as she felt the clogging in her throat, making it hard to speak. It *would* be fine, even if it didn't feel like it.

Tasha promised her mom, after all, that she'd be good, when Mom had first been admitted to the hospital. She hadn't known then that it was going to be the last words they'd speak. After all, so many people had gotten COVID and been just fine. No one had thought Tasha's mom would be one of the people who got sick and never got better.

But it didn't matter why Tasha had said she'd be good. A promise was a promise, and Tasha wasn't going to be trouble. She was lucky to have a place with people who were her family, even if she didn't know them at all. Well, at least one person who felt like family. She'd only known Ms. Washington for five minutes, but she could tell that she was kind.

John, on the other hand . . . Tasha was starting to understand why Mom had always sighed and said it was a long story when she'd asked about her dad. It had been Tasha's mom's way of avoiding telling her the truth, one that Tasha, she realized, had always suspected:

John was kind of a jerk.

Tasha put her backpack on the dresser and mustered up a smile for Ms. Washington. "Can we try those cookies now?"

Ms. Washington beamed back at her. "That's a fantastic idea."

Later than night, after Tasha had brushed her teeth and put on the new pajamas that were not hers but were clean and soft, she lay in bed, unable to sleep in the strange room.

Outside in the living room came the sounds of a talk show of some sort. When Tasha cracked open the bedroom door, she could see Ms. Washington in her recliner, snoring. She crept to the bookshelf and grabbed the book she had seen earlier: *A Guide to Southern Myths and Legends*.

It was better than nothing.

Tasha pulled the book light her mom had given her for her last birthday out of her backpack, clipped it onto the top of the cover, and began reading. The book wasn't bad—it turned out to be a bunch of short stories, most of them about ghosts and monsters. On weekends when she didn't have to work, Mom would snuggle up next to Tasha on the couch, and they'd watch horror movies. Tasha didn't really like scary movies—she liked movies about dragons better, and if she was being honest, she didn't much like those moments in every horror movie when some scary monster would jump out of the shadows. But Mom would always say to her, "It's not the things in the dark that scare us—it's the darkness itself. We're most frightened of what we don't know. That's why we *face* our fears, Tash. Then we won't be afraid anymore." Ms. Washington's book reminded Tasha of those days on the couch.

Tears brimmed at her eyes, and this time, Tasha didn't blink them away. She kept reading even as she began to yawn widely. By the time she'd finished a story about the four different types of swamp witches, her eyes finally felt heavy, and as she closed the book and tucked it under her bed, the heavy grief she carried subsided enough that she could finally get some sleep.

Tasha woke early, the sunshine coming through the window warm on her face. The trailer had air-conditioning, so the room wasn't too hot, but there was a damp stickiness to the air that promised an unbearable day ahead.

Even though she could've slept another hour or two, Tasha climbed out of bed and made her way to the kitchen. She wasn't sure what was expected of her yet, and she didn't want to get in trouble for sleeping too long.

She found Ms. Washington still in her recliner in the living room, the TV blaring *The Price Is Right*. The sight caused a lump to form in Tasha's throat. Her mom had liked *The Price Is Right* as well. She suddenly wished she'd stayed in bed a little longer.

Ms. Washington turned around in the chair and

gave her a smile. "Morning, sunshine. Your daddy is already at work, but he left you an envelope with some pocket money. Just in case you needed it."

"Is there a corner store here?" Tasha asked. Her mom used to leave her money for the corner store when things with money were good. It wasn't often.

"No, but we can ride into town later today and go to the Walmart. How about some breakfast? There's milk and cereal, or I can make bacon if you'd like."

"Cereal is fine," Tasha said. She went to the cupboard and poured a bowl, and she'd just covered it all in milk when the wail of sirens cut through the early morning calm.

"Oh, that sounds close," Ms. Washington said. She hauled herself out of the recliner and opened the front door. Too-bright sunlight poured into the trailer.

Tasha went to look out too, as she scooped Cocoa Bits into her mouth. An ambulance and two cop cars pulled past slowly, lights flashing. She had barely noticed how close the trailers were when she'd arrived the day before, but now she realized that there was only about six feet separating each one. While Ms. Washington's trailer was well maintained, most of the trailers in the park were old aluminum things, with scrubby patches of grass or concrete patios in the space between trailers. The park seemed like the kind of place where people went when they gave up. Tasha's mom had once told Tasha that the most important thing was to never give up, but seeing how the trailers stretched out, sad and dilapidated, made her miss the apartment where she and her mom had lived last. At least they'd had nice grass there.

The ambulance came to a stop three trailers down, in front of a sickly green mobile home covered with rust and dents.

"Well, that's no good," Ms. Washington muttered.

"What's happening?" Tasha asked, chewing quickly so that she wasn't talking with a mouth full of food. She didn't want Ms. Washington to think she had bad manners.

"Not sure, but that's Old Harold's trailer. He's been sick lately. I hope he's okay." After another long look out of the screen door, Ms. Washington eased the front door closed. "Let's leave that to the professionals," she said, her voice soft as though she just remembered Tasha was there.

Tasha went back to the table, setting down her nearly empty bowl. Seeing the ambulance had stolen her appetite. When her mom got sick, gasping and struggling to breathe, Tasha had called 911 and an

27

ambulance like the one outside had appeared. It was the last time Tasha had seen her mom outside of the hospital, lying on a stretcher and being wheeled out to the ambulance as Mrs. Flanagan watched out of her window.

On the TV, a woman guessed the wrong price for macaroni and cheese and missed out on winning a car. Suddenly Tasha felt like she needed to escape the trailer.

"Am I allowed to go outside?" she asked,

Ms. Washington watched Tasha for a long moment before nodding. "That's a good idea. There's a playground you might like up near the entrance to the park. Be careful walking on the main road, though. There's a high school boy in lot seventy-two who likes to drag race with his friends sometimes. Although I suppose with all of the police out there he's not about to get up to any nonsense."

Tasha slipped on her flip-flops, which had been left next to the door, and headed out into the too-hot morning still wearing her pajamas. The heat was nearly a physical presence, the air heavy and the sun scorching. But it was still better than being stuck with an old woman she didn't know in a too-small space. Tasha didn't even blame John for escaping the trailer. She would've as well if she had some place else to be.

Tasha shook her head. She shouldn't think that way. Ms. Washington was her grandma, and she was trying her best. Harder than John was, anyway. So Tasha had to try too, even if it was weird.

The grass around the trailer was cut short, and the blades poked at the sides of her feet as she bent down to run her fingers over the marigolds Ms. Washington kept in her yard. Maybe if Tasha asked nicely, they could plant something blue. She liked blue flowers, especially morning glories. They'd had a pot of morning glories growing on the balcony of their apartment, but John had said the pot was too heavy to bring. Tasha thought the trailer would look better with some morning glories growing up the side.

The flashing lights were far down the road, but there was a playground in the same direction, so Tasha made her way to a jungle gym, which crouched near the entrance to the park like a cat on the prowl.

Ms. Washington's trailer was number thirty-nine, the numbers stuck on the front of the aluminum siding. Tasha studied the trailers on either side of the road as she walked. Some looked older, covered in aluminum siding like Ms. Washington's trailer, while others were newer with exteriors that looked like some kind of wood. No matter where she looked, though, everything was just a little run-down, as if the world had forgotten about the trailer park and its residents. Just like John had forgotten about her and Mom.

The thought was too much to bear, so Tasha turned her attention to the drama unfolding in front of Old Harold's place, slowing her pace as she passed by. A police officer, his pale face twisted in a scowl, took notes while a medic in a dark blue polo murmured in low tones. They seemed to be arguing about something. But they both turned at the sound of a stretcher being brought out of the trailer. There was a sheet over the person on the gurney, the wheels unfolding as they hit the dirt and gravel road that ran the length of the park.

For a moment Tasha was back to that terrible day her mother went to the hospital, helpless and afraid and hoping that everything would be okay.

The medics pushed the gurney toward the ambulance, and Tasha was just about to be on her way when one of the wheels hit a rock. The person underneath the sheet was strapped down, but the hand that fell out from under the sheet was not.

It was like nothing she had ever seen before. The

limb was bloody and red, bits of bone and tendon poking through. Tasha didn't know what she was seeing at first. It looked just like the anatomy book her mom had once let her check out of the library. Sinew and fat, bone and cartilage, bloody and horrible.

"Hey, watch that!" the medic talking to the cop said, her gaze meeting Tasha's for a moment. "For the love of Pete, be careful."

The police officer was looking at Tasha now, and so she started walking again, ducking her head as she passed the adults. She wasn't thinking about them, though. Instead, her mind kept replaying the sight of that arm, the way the muscles looked ropey and defined, and the bright white hue of the bony fingers. It looked like someone had turned the arm inside out. Or had peeled the skin right off.

She had just reached the wood-chip-covered play area when she felt a curious shift in her middle. She bent over and threw up Cocoa Bits all over the playground.

It was still less gross than that skinless hand.

Once her stomach was empty, every last Cocoa Bit in the wood chips and dirt at the edge of the playground, Tasha felt better. She tried to convince herself that what she'd seen was normal, not weird at all. Ms. Washington had said Old Harold had been sick; there was probably some sort of illness that could do that to a person's body. Or maybe it was a long time between when he died and when the ambulance had been called; perhaps some animal, like a possum, had found him and—

No, Tasha thought. It would be easier if she just stopped thinking about it altogether.

Tasha pushed the horrible image to the side and took in the playground before her. It wasn't a bad setup, with a jungle gym, a couple of cool tire things, and even some swings. It was too hot to try climbing through the tunnels on the main structure, and she was probably too big for that little-kid stuff anyway, but the swings looked appealing. Tasha sat on one and kicked her feet forward before leaning back and keeping her legs straight like her mom had taught her so many years ago.

You've got to be patient. Kick, lean, kick, lean . . . that's it! Just like that.

All the back-and-forth was starting to make her feel nauseated again. She jumped off the swing, the pieces of wood that lined the playground poking her feet through her flip-flops. There wasn't much more to see, and no one around, so she didn't know what else she could do but head back to the trailer. At least it would be nice and cool inside.

The walk back seemed much shorter than the walk to the playground had been. All the vehicles that had been in front of Old Harold's trailer were gone now. A cat slinked out from between the panels of skirting that surrounded the base of the trailer and watched Tasha with suspicious eyes, like she was somehow intruding on the feline's day. She called to the cat to see if it would come to her, but it only stared for a moment before lifting its tail in the air and sauntering off.

"I didn't want to pet you anyway," Tasha grumbled.

When Tasha opened the door to the trailer, cool air welcomed her back, giving her sweaty skin a brief chill as she stepped inside. Ms. Washington smiled at her before turning back to the TV where a woman was yelling at someone who she said was the father of her baby, telling him that he was nothing more than a deadbeat. Tasha had never heard the word before but she liked it. Maybe that was the problem with John. What if he was just a deadbeat? It made Tasha wonder what it had been like when her mom got pregnant with her. Had John been like the man on the TV, insisting that the baby wasn't his?

"How was the playground?" Ms. Washington asked, dragging Tasha's thoughts back to the present.

"Hot," Tasha said, plopping on the couch. She wasn't sure how to ask the question she wanted to ask, so she just asked it. "Did my mom get a DNA test when I was born?"

Ms. Washington laughed a little. "Why? You trying to evaluate your options?"

Tasha shook her head. "No, that's not what I meant." But in truth, she was kind of wondering if perhaps there might be someone else out there who could be her dad. There had been a kid at school last year who found out that his dad wasn't really his dad after his parents divorced, and Tasha remembered the way he'd come to school every day after, like his entire world had exploded. She wished she'd been nicer to that kid, sat with him at lunch or something. She kind of knew how he felt now.

"There was no need," Ms. Washington said, shifting in her chair. "Your mom and dad dated for a long time before she got pregnant with you. I actually thought they'd get married. But your daddy, well, he's always convinced there's something better around the corner."

"What do you mean, something better?"

Ms. Washington's expression pinched, like she'd just smelled a fart, and Tasha regretted asking the question. But who else could tell her the truth? Her mom was gone and John was . . . wherever John was. There was nothing of him in the trailer—no shoes, no pictures. Tasha had the feeling that he was more gone than he was around. Was he even going to take care of her? Or was he just expecting his mom to do that?

Finally, Ms. Washington said, "You don't need to worry about any of that. You're young, leave those kinds of worries to the grown-ups."

Tasha wouldn't get to say anything else, because there was a knock on the trailer door then, heavy and insistent. She climbed to her feet before Ms. Washington could get up and opened the door, the bright sunshine making her eyes water as they adjusted.

It was an elderly woman. She had wispy white curls and was bird thin, her arms like sticks, and she held a small, fluffy black-and-white dog. The house-coat she wore billowed around her like a tent. Her skin was pale and Tasha tried not to be grossed out by the blue veins crisscrossing her arms and exposed legs. She was only half-successful.

"Oh, you must be the granddaughter," the woman said. "I'm Greta. Your grandma home?"

"Let her in," Ms. Washington shouted from behind Tasha, and she stepped back as Ms. Greta climbed the steps slowly. When she finally gained the landing, she entered the trailer like she belonged there, and Tasha closed the door behind her.

"Well, Old Harold is dead," Ms. Greta said, shuf-fling over to the couch. The little dog in Ms. Greta's arms didn't even move, and Tasha couldn't tell whether it was even real until it lifted its head, sniffed at her, and then rested its head once more in the crook of the old woman's arms.

"Greta! Have a little tact," Ms. Washington said, looking pointedly at Tasha, who had taken a seat in the chair beside them.

"What?" Ms. Greta said, and then her expression softened. "Oh, I'm sorry to hear about your momma," she said, leaning over to pat Tasha's bare thigh with an icy hand. "But Old Harold was, well, old. Not nearly as tragic as your story."

Tasha didn't like the idea that her dead mom was somehow "her story," but she did appreciate the old woman's apology. "Was, uh, Mr. Harold sick?" Tasha asked, unable to get the memory of that skinless arm out of her head.

"He's been ill for a while," Ms. Washington said with a nod. "Heart problems, I believe."

"The old codger smoked for years," Ms. Greta said. "Used to puff on these cigars and the stink of them would float from his front porch and fill up my house. Fredo here hated it, would bark at him every time we smelled him. I live down by where he did," she added for Tasha's benefit. "You'll see me out with Fredo here every now and again."

Fredo snorted in his sleep. He obviously had no opinion on the matter.

"Did anyone call Harold's daughter?" Ms. Washington asked. "I think Susan is her name?"

"As soon as I saw the ambulance," Ms. Greta said with a sniff. "That's the third one this month! It's

37

going to be a busy summer." She yawned widely and hummed a little as she finished. "I have not slept a wink these past few nights. I think I have a possum under my house. There's this scratching at all hours!"

The conversation turned to the problem with getting Shady Pines to hire someone to take care of the rodent problem, and Tasha turned back to the television, which was now running a show with people trying to answer questions to win money. She zoned out until Ms. Greta creakily climbed to her feet and declared she had to get back before her stories came on.

Tasha watched as the woman left, and as soon as the door shut her grandmother exhaled loudly. "My goodness, that woman can talk," she said with a small laugh.

"Have a lot of people died here recently?" Tasha asked. It was hard to think about anything but the medics taking the stretcher out to the ambulance and the dead man's hand. And it was hard not to think about Mom, being wheeled out of their apartment with an oxygen tube stuck in her nose, looking tired and drawn. Tasha didn't want to live in a place that reminded her of that.

"No, sweetie, not a lot," Ms. Washington said. "But people do die here. There are a lot of older people in the park, and old people get sick and pass away. Are you upset because of the ambulance?"

Tasha nodded and Ms. Washington slapped her hands against her thighs.

"Tell you what, why don't we go out to lunch and then go to the Walmart? You can get some things to decorate your room, take your mind off of the drama from this morning."

That sounded a lot better than sitting around watching game shows and the petty drama of other people's lives. "Do we need to wait until John—my dad comes home?" Tasha asked.

Ms. Washington's face fell for a moment before she covered it with a smile. "Your daddy is a busy man. He works long hours, and when work's done . . . Well, we shouldn't wait around on him."

"But doesn't he even want to—" Tasha began but cut herself off. She hated how her voice sounded—soft, whiny—and she swallowed hard at the lump in her throat. She wanted to be somewhere else, with someone else. She wanted to be home with her mom, eating ice cream from the carton and laughing at internet videos of animals. She didn't want to be in this stupid trailer, abandoned by a father who would rather watch basketball with his friends than get to know his daughter.

At least when he'd left the first time, she'd been a baby. She hadn't known to be upset.

Ms. Washington's expression shifted. "Tasha, you're going to have to be patient with your daddy. He tries, he really does. He's just not very good at taking care of other people. He tends to forget he isn't the center of the universe. But don't worry. I know he'll come around."

Tasha could hear the meaning behind the words. John hadn't cared that she existed before her mom died, and if Mom hadn't called him, he might not have ever thought about her again. Tasha felt her hands curling into fists. Why did her mom have to die? Why did she have to get sent to live with a man who didn't care about her in a trailer park full of dying people?

But when she looked again at Ms. Washington, Tasha pushed those feelings to the side and mustered a smile.

"I like Walmart," she said. "Let's do it."

John might not care that what he did hurt other people. But Ms. Washington was a nice old lady who had made cookies for Tasha to make her feel at home. She wouldn't do anything to make Ms. Washington sad.

Even if Tasha was getting the feeling that her dad really was a deadbeat.

Tasha's life took on an uneasy rhythm over the next couple of days. In the morning she got up whenever she felt like it—it was summer vacation, after all—and lay in bed reading Ms. Washington's book of southern myths and legends until her stomach sent her in search of food. Then she'd eat breakfast and sit on the couch and stare at the TV until it was time for lunch. She was surprised by how many hours she could fill, reading and watching an endless parade of daytime television. In the evenings, Ms. Washington would make dinner, which became the highlight of Tasha's day. It turned out her grandmother was a really good cook.

She didn't see much of John. He came by the day after their Walmart trip to give Tasha pocket money before making excuses about working double shifts and disappearing once more. Tasha had the feeling he was avoiding her, which was fine. She didn't want to talk to him much, either. Tasha had learned from her grandmother's daytime TV shows that deadbeats were a regular part of life and a waste of her time. So she decided she wasn't going to worry about John anymore. Instead, she put her hurt feelings in the same imaginary box she kept her thoughts about her mom, pushing them down and away so they could be ignored.

Four days after Tasha arrived at the trailer park, Ms. Washington put her hands on her hips and looked at her like she was a problem that needed solving. "I have seen you read that same book every single day this week. The haints and witches of the south cannot be that interesting."

Tasha hefted the book and shrugged. "I like witches. They're cool."

"I don't think you should be filling your head with that stuff all day. You're going to give yourself nightmares. You haven't been outside much since you got here—why don't you go out and play? There are usually kids on the playground around this time of day."

This, to Tasha, sounded like the worst thing she'd heard in a while. And she'd had a pretty awful year.

Something of her distaste must have shown on her

face, because Ms. Washington's expression softened. "Listen, if you go play outside today, I'll take you into town tomorrow. We can go to the library, find you some books that are a bit more appropriate. But you don't want to waste your summer vacation hanging out with an old lady, right?" She smiled.

"Okay," Tasha mumbled. She slid her feet into her flip-flops and headed out into the heat.

The sun was already punishing the landscape as Tasha made her way, reluctantly, back to the playground. She was nearly there when a voice called out to her.

"Are you going to throw up again?"

"Huh?" Tasha said, looking here and there to see where the voice had come from.

"I saw you puke a couple days ago. When the ambulance was here."

Tasha blinked in the hot sunshine until she could make out a girl, standing nearby in the shade of one of the trailers. She was white, tall, and skinny, with straight blond hair, and she had grime smeared across the side of her face and under her fingernails like she'd been digging in the dirt.

Tasha studied the girl with distrust. She wasn't used to kids randomly talking to her. People in Atlanta usually just ignored each other unless there was a reason to chat. And when they did, they usually weren't asking such prying questions. She didn't quite know what to do with the girl giving her a gap-toothed grin.

"You hear me?" the girl asked.

Tasha nodded.

The girl peered at Tasha curiously. "You talk?"

"Yes, I can talk," Tasha said with a huff. She didn't want the girl to get the better of her, especially as she was a bit embarrassed that she'd apparently seen Tasha vomit.

The girl held up her hands. "I'm just asking because I got a cousin who doesn't talk, on account of being autistic. There's nothing wrong with not talking, you know? I'm Ellie."

Tasha was already thinking up an excuse about her grandma calling her, anything to get away. But the girl gave her another smile.

"Do you want a Popsicle? We've got grape and cherry. We had orange as well but I ate all of those."

Tasha looked from the playground, which seemed blistering hot in the sunshine, to Ellie, who sat in the shade of an awning next to her trailer, one of the nicer ones with the fake wood on the outside. The girl's expression was friendly and open, her pale eyebrows almost swallowed by her bangs, and a Popsicle in the shade definitely seemed like a better idea.

Maybe Tasha should try to get to know some of the people here. It was what her mom would've told her to do. "Grape, please. Thanks."

Ellie dashed off to the back of the trailer and Tasha moved from the road that ran through the trailer park and into the shade. The relief was immediate.

Ellie came back with two Popsicles for each of them. "They're kind of small. But you'll have to eat them fast before they melt." She stripped the wrappers off both of hers and shoved them in either side of her mouth, like walrus tusks. When she spoke around them, it was nearly unintelligible. "You're new, aren't you? What's your name and where do you live?"

"I'm Tasha. I just moved in with my grandmother." Tasha opened just one of the Popsicles. Ellie's method seemed like a sure way to end up with sticky hands.

"Which trailer?" Ellie asked, slurping at her Popsicles as she pulled them from her mouth.

"We're trailer thirty-nine."

"Ms. Washington's place? She's the nicest old lady in the whole park. She let me plant some flowers in her dirt."

"Those are your marigolds?" Tasha asked. She bit

into the Popsicle, the cold making her teeth hurt. But the pain was bracing, chasing away the sudden surge of possessiveness she felt at hearing that Ms. Washington was so close with Ellie.

"Yeah, and I also planted other plants around her trailer."

"Why can't you grow flowers here?" Tasha asked, before she realized that where they were standing was covered entirely in concrete. "Oh, never mind."

"Yeah, my aunt's boyfriend got me some flowerpots, but only the tomatoes really grow good in those. You want some cherry tomatoes? I mean, when they're ripe. They're still small right now. Anyway, Ms. Washington asked if I'd like to help her plant around her trailer. It's like she knew I wanted to grow something. She's nice like that. You're real lucky."

Tasha took another bite of her Popsicle, sucking on it until it melted into juice. "I didn't even know Ms. Washington until I found out she was my grandma a few days ago. My mom died. So now I have to live here."

Ellie's lips turned downward; she looked just like a sad emoji. "I'm so sorry. Do you want another Popsicle?"

For some reason, that made Tasha laugh. Not

because she was happy, but because this girl was trying to fix the sadness that had settled deep in Tasha's middle with a Popsicle. Still, Ellie was trying. "No, thanks," Tasha said. "I still have to eat the second one."

"That's 'cause you eat slow," Ellie said, brandishing her two bare Popsicle sticks. "So, is that why you got sick the other day? Because of your mom? I used to get stomachaches a lot after my mom left, but my aunt took me to the doctor and she said it was probably stress. I guess having a mom die would give you a whole lot of stress."

Tasha shook her head, and just like that she was thinking about Old Harold's gross hand again. "No. Actually, I . . . saw the dead body. Of the old man who died that day. His hand looked . . . weird. Like his skin had fallen off. I think he maybe had some kind of disease."

Ellie's eyes widened and she shook her head slowly. "You saw Mr. Harold's dead body? Did you also see the ghost too?"

Tasha froze mid-bite. "Ghost?"

"Oh yeah. I saw it slinking around Mr. Harold's trailer before he died. You've got to be careful, especially at night. That's when it comes out. Which is why I wear this." Ellie pointed to a bracelet with a large charm in the middle. It looked like a staring blue eye. "The Evil Eye keeps murder ghosts away."

Tasha didn't quite know what to say, so she just nodded slowly. "Mm-hmm."

Ellie narrowed her eyes. "You don't believe me. I get it. I thought I was imagining it at first too. But I can prove it's real. Last night I saw the murder ghost again, by the marsh. It snatched up the cat who used to live under Mr. Harold's trailer. There was this smell, just like death, and then the cat was yowling and . . ." Ellie trailed off, her eyes wide with fear. "I can show you where it happened."

A deep sense of discomfort began to bloom in Tasha's chest. She just met this girl and she was already talking about things like "murder ghosts"? Was Tasha just supposed to pretend like she believed her?

"Ghosts aren't real," Tasha said, her voice low. "And if they were, Ms. Washington has a book about southern myths and legends, and while there are lots of different kinds of ghosts—they're called 'haints'— there aren't any that murder people like that. Or cats. If there were, it would be in the book."

"You have to let me show you the cat the murder ghost killed. Then you'll see. It's not natural, no matter what that book of yours says. Come on." With that, Ellie took off down the street.

Tasha hesitated. She didn't have to follow the girl. The playground was just a couple of trailers away. She could waste some time there before going home and forgetting all about Ellie, murder ghosts, and dead cats.

But part of her was curious. And even if Ellie seemed a bit strange, Tasha realized she liked the idea of having someone to spend time with, rather than watching the same mindless TV shows day in and day out. Ms. Washington had friends, after all, even if it was just Ms. Greta coming over every morning to gossip and complain about her kids.

Ellie stopped in the middle of the dusty road. "Are you coming?" she demanded. There was a fierce look on her face, and Tasha half thought the girl might drag her along if she said no.

So she opened her second Popsicle, licked off all the melty parts, and trudged after Ellie.

The two girls walked the main road that ran through the trailer park. Ellie was silent, and there was something in the set of her jaw that gave Tasha an uneasy mix of feelings—afraid of what the girl might have to show her, but unable to resist finding out.

Ellie led them right to the edge of an undeveloped area beyond the far back end of the trailer park. The grass was verdant and high, and water glimmered between tall blades. There were no trailers, and not too far away a wide creek made its slow way off into some nearby trees. There was a loud splash from somewhere off to their left, and Tasha began to worry just a bit. This was the kind of spot that might have alligators.

"What is this place?" Tasha asked. The slow sound of frogs croaking filled the air, and it felt as if they were a world away from the trailer park just behind them.

"This is the marsh. When my mom still lived with us, we used to come back here and go fishing. I caught a catfish once, but it was too small to eat so we let it go. But I haven't seen many fish here lately. Not since the murder ghost." Ellie wrapped her arms around her middle despite the heat. "It sneaks off into those trees after eating people."

"Wait, this ghost is *eating* people?" Tasha asked. Her Popsicle was gone and she had no place to put the stick, so she held it in her sticky hand. "Really?"

"Maybe you haven't gotten to that part in your book yet," Ellie said, unbothered by Tasha's skepticism. "I don't think it eats, like, their whole body, though. More like it sucks out their soul, and then they die."

Tasha looked around at the birds, the lily pads peeking in between the grasses. A few lilies floated in the fetid water, which smelled a little like dead fish. Even with the eeriness of the book of southern legends plaguing her thoughts, Tasha still couldn't see how a ghost like the one Ellie was describing could be real. A swamp witch? Maybe . . .

But her realistic concerns were a bit more pressing at the moment. "Are there alligators around here?" Tasha asked. A mosquito hovered around her face and she swiped at it in annoyance.

"Sometimes, but that's not what we're here to see. Come on, I'll show you."

Ellie started walking along the edge of the water and Tasha followed. She was in it now, and she might as well see it through. The grass was deep and the ground soft close to the water, so much so that Tasha's flip-flops sank deep into the mud. Each step made a sucking sound as she pulled her foot out.

The smell hit Tasha first, a deep and sickly sweet scent. She didn't quite know what it was, but she'd smelled it before, usually when they were driving along back roads in the summertime. It smelled like a trash can left too long on the curb, putrid and nauseating.

Ellie stopped and turned around to wave Tasha up. "It's over there. Can you see it?" she said, her voice little more than a whisper.

The stink was nearly overwhelming in this spot. "What smells so bad?" Tasha asked.

Ellie just pointed.

It took a moment for Tasha to figure out what she was looking at. At first she thought it was an abandoned stuffie covered in rice, but then she realized it was a dead thing. And it was swarming with maggots.

She took half a step back, her stomach going queasy all over again. "What is that?"

"Mr. Harold's cat," Ellie said, looking as uncomfortable as Tasha felt. "The day he died I tried to catch it, because I didn't think anyone else was going to take care of it, but it ran off. I followed it here on my bike, because cats are fast, and I saw something come out of the water with thin claws and long hair that was wet and dripping. I thought it was a really skinny woman at first, because of the hair. But then I realized it looked just like the slinking shadow I'd seen a few times before, including right outside Mr. Harold's trailer. The way it moved was weird, more like a bug than a person. It grabbed the cat and just—" Ellie swallowed, shaking her head. "The cat made this awful sound and . . . Yeah, murder ghost."

"Are you serious?" Tasha said. Her brain refused to actually hear what Ellie was saying.

"It smelled so bad. Before I could even move, it just . . . disappeared back into the water. You believe me now, right?" Ellie said, her expression hopeful. "Whatever this ghost is, Mr. Harold was definitely killed by it. Now I'm worried that other old people were as well. My aunt told me that a few of them weren't vaccinated and got COVID, but now I'm not so sure . . ."

Tasha shook her head, refusing to hear Ellie's words. She already had enough going on in her life.

Why did she have to deal with skinless hands and dead cats and weird girls talking about death?

Tasha took another step backward, then another, and another. "No, that's not . . . no. Things don't just come out of the water, killing cats. Ghosts aren't real. You know what is, though? People getting sick and dying. Even when they're not old." Grief nipped at Tasha, the memory of her mom gasping for air, but she pushed it aside, leaning into anger instead. "Leave me alone."

She turned and stalked back the way they'd come, the white wriggling mess of the dead cat an image she wouldn't soon forget. Ellie yelled something after her, but Tasha was done. Ghosts or not, she didn't want anything to do with this girl who spent her time running around looking at dead things.

She'd rather watch *The Price Is Right*.

Tasha stomped all the way back to the trailer, and it was only after she'd reached the front step that she realized she was still gripping the stick from the Popsicle Ellie had so generously given her. The wood had snapped in half.

Ms. Washington was vacuuming when Tasha entered, the ancient machine wheezing as it ran across the threadbare rug. Tasha paused on the threshold, her flip-flops still caked in mud. As she removed them, Ms. Washington stopped the vacuum.

"I can do that, if you'd like," Tasha said.

Ms. Washington shook her head. "Why don't you dust?" She pointed to a nearby caddy of cleaning supplies, an old-fashioned feather duster resting on top. "Your daddy is going to be home for dinner tonight around six, and I want to make sure the place looks nice. I think he'll be bringing Kim."

"Kim?" Tasha asked, getting the duster and giving the top of the TV a half-hearted swipe. She remembered the name but couldn't place it.

"That's his girlfriend. He texted, said that he wants you to meet her."

"Is she nice?" Tasha asked, not sure how she felt about meeting another person after her disastrous morning with Ellie.

"She is," Ms. Washington said, but something about her tone made Tasha turn and look at her grandmother. The woman's face revealed nothing. "Let's just get this done so we can wash up before they arrive."

They spent the rest of the afternoon cleaning. They wiped down windows and spritzed air freshener, and then Tasha took a shower and made sure her curls were pulled back just right. Tasha's mom had always called her curls her crowning glory, and Tasha wanted to make sure they looked the best they could. Not for John or Kim, but for Ms. Washington. Tasha didn't really care if John came around or not, but it was clear Ms. Washington loved her son. She was practically sparkling at the idea of him coming for dinner, and judging by the amount of food she was making, this was going to be a feast. Ms. Washington had collards simmering on the stove, the fatback in them making the entire trailer smell delicious, and considering the numerous pie plates on the counter, Ms. Washington was going to fry some catfish to go along with the greens. Tasha was mostly excited about the macaroni and cheese sitting in the oven. She liked the gooey mac and cheese better than the baked mac and cheese, but any mac and cheese was better than no mac and cheese, and her mouth watered just thinking about it.

Just before six o'clock, Ms. Washington began frying the fish. Tasha sat in the living room reading her big book of southern monsters while the older woman worked.

At seven, John and Kim still hadn't arrived.

At seven thirty, Ms. Washington seemed to deflate, and took plates out of the cupboard with a sigh. "We should eat before this fish gets any drier," she said, a note of annoyance in her voice.

They dished up the food, which was good but wasn't as good as if they'd eaten it when it was first ready. The fish was indeed a little dry, the mac and cheese as well, and the greens were too soupy. But everything still tasted good, and Tasha ate every single bite that Ms. Washington put on her plate. And then she asked for seconds.

"This is good," Tasha said. The sad slump to Ms.

Washington's shoulders made Tasha determined to try and turn the evening around. John might be a deadbeat, but she wasn't.

And neither was Ms. Washington. She didn't deserve to be treated so poorly.

After they were finished eating, Tasha helped do the dishes, and then Ms. Washington shooed her from the kitchen. Tasha decided that she would spend the rest of the evening reading her book of southern legends, looking for any information about haints that would do the sort of things Ellie claimed. The girl's assertion that it was real no matter what Tasha thought had stuck in her craw in a way she couldn't explain.

Tasha read through most of the book, flipping the pages quickly. After a while, she started feeling sleepy, and she still hadn't found anything about "murder ghosts" or anything like what Ellie had told her had happened. But she had been reading quickly, and there were still a few chapters left. Tasha decided she would go back and read through more carefully after she was finished with the book.

The house was quiet by the time Tasha got in bed and turned out the light. John and Kim had never shown, and Ms. Washington had spent all day cooking and getting the house ready. If that had been Tasha, she would've been mad about it, but she got the feeling that maybe this hadn't been the first time this had happened to Ms. Washington.

It was beginning to explain why Tasha's mom had never really talked about her dad. Who wanted to admit that they'd once dated a deadbeat? Tasha yawned and closed her eyes.

A moment later, she heard a scrabbling noise at the window, like something was trying to get in. She rolled over to look at the partially opened curtains, but there was nothing.

She considered whether to get up and investigate, but she was finally comfortable in the nest of her new bed. The day had been long, and if it hadn't been for the book she'd been reading and Ellie's claims of a murder ghost, would Tasha have even worried about the sound?

No, she wouldn't have.

So even though her head was full of southern ghost stories, Tasha rolled over, ignoring the sound. She fell into a fitful sleep moments later, her dreams full of monstrous, skinless cats scratching to get inside.

After her night of fitful sleep, Tasha didn't think about Ellie or swamp ghosts or dead cats again. At least, she tried not to. She instead focused on just getting through the day, which she spent in the living room watching more terrible daytime TV with Ms. Washington. Tasha didn't want to think about her dad at all either, but that was impossible with Ms. Washington bringing him up at every possible moment. She still seemed a bit sad he hadn't shown up to dinner the night before, but as the day went on, there was something more, like she was concerned Tasha was judging him.

And she would be right. Because even though Tasha had never had a father, she could tell that he wasn't doing such a great job.

During *The Price Is Right*, when a man cheered his fiancée on as she tried to win a car, Ms. Washington patted Tasha's hand and said, "You met your father at a bad time. It's hard to distract a man in love." But, Tasha nearly asked, he hadn't been in love every minute for the last twelve years, had he? Because Tasha had been around all that time. If he couldn't find time for her then, or now, maybe it really wasn't about his new girlfriend at all.

But Tasha didn't say anything to Ms. Washington, because in truth, she didn't mind his absence. Like her mom always used to say, you couldn't miss what you never had.

Later that night, Tasha woke to the sound of arguing. It was Ms. Washington and John. Their voices were too muffled to hear exactly what they were saying, but it didn't take a genius to figure it was probably about him being gone all the time.

Tasha just rolled over and went back to sleep. As Mom also used to say, people were who they were. No use in fretting about it.

If Tasha wasn't so sad about her father not being around, she did still have moments of deep sadness whenever she thought too long about Mom. Ms. Washington had helped her pick out a frame for a picture the social worker in Atlanta had printed off her mom's phone for her. In it, Tasha and her mom were smiling, standing in front of the penguin exhibit at the zoo. Tasha hadn't wanted to go that day, she remembered—she thought she was too old for kid stuff like that. But her mother had shaken her head and said, "You are *never* too old for the zoo." And Mom had been right. It was a great day, and now that moment was frozen forever on her dresser, right next to the box that held her mom's ashes.

Each night, Tasha would lie in the dark and look at that picture, even though it was too dim to make out the details. Those were the only times she would let herself cry. Ms. Washington was so nice and had so much to worry about, Tasha didn't want to upset her.

Sadness or no, it was still summer, and Tasha was going to take advantage of school being out for the next two months. That meant reading every book she could find. Instead of worrying about her absent father or the well of grief in her heart, she buried herself in the books she grabbed from the living room. She finished the book of southern legends and moved on to another book about the most haunted places in the South. Despite Ellie's claims, Shady Pines Estates was not on the list.

Tasha didn't know why what Ellie told her about the murder ghost still bothered her, but it did. Maybe because a trailer park seemed like the last place a ghost would haunt. Beautiful old mansion in the woods? Yes, that seemed about right. But a dusty trailer park full of mostly old people? Why would a ghost want to hang around this place? It didn't make sense. And it wasn't like ghosts even existed anyway!

But she couldn't understand why Ellie would lie to someone she just met.

"Did you just finish that book too?" Ms. Washington asked, startling Tasha as she was staring blankly at the final page. Ms. Washington was reading a book of her own—a crime thriller thing she'd gotten from the Walmart that sometimes made her gasp out loud. Since Tasha liked to read so much, Ms. Washington had decided she needed to get better about reading as well, and so after lunch the TV went off and they both read until dinner.

"It's okay, there's plenty more," Tasha said. In truth, though, the rest of Ms. Washington's shelf were mostly self-help books that looked boring, and mysteries with blood and chalk outlines of bodies on the covers.

Ms. Washington seemed to read her mind. "Oh, you don't want to read any of those things. I promised you a trip to the library. Let's go see what's new."

And so Tasha found herself at the local library. Ms. Washington disappeared into the mystery section while Tasha wandered the aisles looking at the spines. She'd always loved libraries; no matter where they'd lived her mom had always made sure they had a library card, and Tasha had come to see libraries as a sort of sacred place.

So when she saw Ellie running through the stacks like a wild animal, her stomach sank. The last thing she wanted to do was talk about imaginary murder ghosts.

Tasha ducked down another aisle, trying to avoid Ellie, and ran right into a young woman pulling a book from a shelf.

"Oh!" she said, dropping the stack of books in her arms.

"Oh no," Tasha said, and bent down to help pick them up. "I'm sorry."

"It's not a problem," the woman said kindly. "But you should probably watch where you're going. There are a lot of older folks who come to the library."

Tasha nodded. "They could get hurt."

"That's true—but they can also be pretty mean when someone bumps into them," the woman said with a smile. "Don't ask me how I know."

"Tasha, where did—" Ms. Washington said, coming around the aisle. "Oh! Kim!"

"Ms. Washington!" the woman said, rising. "It's so nice to see you."

Tasha blinked at her from where she still knelt on the floor. So this was Kim, John's girlfriend and the reason he couldn't be bothered to come by the trailer. She was pretty, Tasha begrudgingly admitted. She was white, and her long brown hair was twisted up on top of her head and held in place with a jeweled hair clip. She wore a dress with a pattern of kittens chasing balls of yarn.

"I see you met Tasha, John's daughter," Ms. Washington said. Tasha got the feeling Ms. Washington didn't care for Kim, but it wasn't just because of the strange tone that had entered the old woman's voice. She was giving Kim a look like she was gum Ms. Washington had just found on the bottom of her shoe.

"This is Tasha?" Kim said, her smile somehow brightening. "It's great to meet you."

"Kim is a seamstress," Ms. Washington said.

Tasha nodded, remembering. "Did you make your dress?" she asked, because that sounded like the polite thing to say.

"I did! Do you like it?" Kim asked with a gentle smile. Tasha was having trouble picturing her with

John. She seemed too nice—not nice like John had been, but a real kind of nice, like Ms. Washington.

"I do," Tasha said.

"Well then, I shall make you one of your own. I'll have to take your measurements first. Perhaps you can come have dinner with your dad and me some night."

"Speaking of dinner, what happened to you and John on Tuesday?" Ms. Washington asked. "Tasha and I spent all day getting ready for you to come over."

Kim frowned prettily and shook her head. "I'm not sure what you're talking about?"

"John said he was bringing you over for dinner. He told me you were craving catfish and, well, I make the best," Ms. Washington said, though there was hesitation in her voice.

"Ma'am, I promise that if I'd known you were making catfish, I would've been there with bells on," Kim said. "I've had to work late all week for a rush job on some bridesmaids' dresses. I'm not exactly sure what John has been up to, but he didn't say anything about dinner this past week."

Ms. Washington pursed her lips in displeasure and sighed, and Tasha shifted from foot to foot, uncomfortable. She couldn't tell if her grandmother was annoyed with John or with his girlfriend, but Tasha couldn't see how it could be Kim. She hadn't even known about the invitation.

"John told me about your mom, Tasha," Kim said, looking at her again. "I'm so sorry you had to go through that. My mom died when I was young, and I know how hard it can be when you're suddenly left alone."

Tasha's eyes stung with unexpected tears, and for a moment she was afraid she would cry if she tried to respond. But then Kim patted her on the shoulder. "If you ever need anyone to talk to about what you're feeling, I'm a pretty good listener. Just tell John and we'll make it happen, okay?"

Tasha nodded mutely.

"Tasha, why don't you go and find something new to read," Ms. Washington said, her voice low, and Tasha's head snapped up. The suggestion sounded more like a command, and Tasha had never heard Ms. Washington talk that way. But Ms. Washington's gaze wasn't on Tasha—it was on Kim. "The two of us need to have a chat."

Kim seemed unbothered by Ms. Washington's words. Instead, she just smiled. "Nice to meet you, Tasha."

Tasha nodded and gave the woman a small smile.

She made her way to the adult fantasy section,

figuring she'd check out the kids' books once she was sure Ellie was gone. But that was when Ellie came running around the corner, careening right toward her. She skidded to a stop when she saw Tasha.

"New kid," Ellie said.

"It's Tasha," she said before turning and walking back toward the kids' section. No sense in avoiding it now; Ellie had seen her.

"Hey!" Ellie called after her, but Tasha just kept walking. Her eyes still felt wet, and she definitely didn't want to deal with Ellie while she thought about Kim. John had never told her he was sorry Mom had died—he didn't even want to talk about it right after it had happened. How could someone so nice be dating *him*?

Tasha had only gone a few steps when the sound of pounding feet came up alongside her.

"Why do you keep running off like that?" Ellie said. "Is it that you're afraid of ghosts?"

"What? No, I just . . . just leave me alone. I have enough to deal with," Tasha said. "Quit being so . . . weird."

Ellie stopped in her tracks. "Weird? I'm trying to be your friend. You said your mom died. I know how much it stinks when you don't have a mom. It's nice to have someone to talk to about serious stuff."

Ellie's kindness in spite of Tasha's insult made her eyes water once more—but no one seemed to understand. Kim and Ellie felt sorry for her because she had a dead mom, Ms. Washington felt bad her dad wasn't around more, but all Tasha wanted was to be left alone. She was *fine*.

"I don't need a friend," Tasha gritted out, fighting back tears. She was afraid that if she started crying, she wouldn't be able to stop. "So stop trying."

Tasha stomped off, and this time Ellie didn't try to follow her.

In her middle, Tasha felt terrible about being so mean to Ellie, but she didn't want to talk about her mom being dead. She didn't want to think about moms at all, really. And Ellie was just too much. All Tasha wanted to do was read books and eat cookies. The last thing she needed in her life was someone who believed in murder ghosts, ate too many Popsicles, and hung out looking at dead, decomposing cats.

Tasha grabbed a couple of fantasy books she hadn't read before from the kids' shelves, not even reading the back to see what they were about, and went to go find Ms. Washington. She could feel Ellie's gaze on her, but Tasha didn't turn around once.

It was better to just get rid of the girl. Even if she had to be mean to do it.

Tasha spent the next week trying to forget about the incident in the library, the deaths in the trailer park, and her dad and his new girlfriend. But that all came crashing down when John showed up at the trailer on a Friday evening, wearing the world's biggest grin.

"Ma, we're going out to dinner," he said as he came through the door, plopping down on the couch before bending over to take his work boots off. It was only the second time Tasha had seen him since she'd moved into the trailer. His presence felt strange and yet he looked so comfortable; it was a bit like finding a bear sitting in your kitchen eating cereal.

But when Ms. Washington spoke, it was as though her son hadn't been absent for the last two weeks. "Out? But I took pork chops out of the freezer," she said from the kitchen, where she was finishing the dishes.

"I know, but . . . well, Kim wants us to get together for a family dinner. She's been nagging me about it since you saw her at the library."

Ms. Washington crossed her arms. "Oh? And what do you think?"

"I agree. You and Tasha spend too much time cooped up in this trailer. It's summer! Let's get out there and enjoy it. Right, kiddo?"

Tasha looked up from where she was curled on her beanbag chair in the corner of the living room reading a book about a finishing school for girls with magic. Ms. Washington had bought the chair from the internet just for Tasha, saying that she needed a fun place to sit. Tasha had worked it into the perfect body-shaped groove, but it had taken her all afternoon, and she didn't really want to move. Especially when Ms. Washington was going to make pork chops.

"Why can't Kim come here?" Tasha asked.

"Because this is special. It's our first dinner together as a real family." John's grin didn't budge as he spoke.

Tasha wanted to point out that John really only seemed to care about family now, when he wanted to get his way. But judging from Ms. Washington's sigh, that would be the wrong thing to say, so Tasha said nothing.

A minute later, they were all piling into John's car—Ms. Washington in the passenger seat and Tasha curled up in the back—and heading into town.

They were going to meet Kim at a buffet place, and John chatted about her the whole time. How excited she was to spend time with them, and how cool she was. Tasha stopped listening and went back to reading. She'd hardly seen her father since he'd picked her up in Atlanta, and she hadn't seen Kim since that day at the library. There was no reason to get excited about a whole lot of hot air. Kim had seemed nice. But then, so had John.

And there were much more interesting things in the pages of her book. Like caticorns—cats with magical horns, like a unicorn.

John eventually parked the car, and they climbed out in front of the restaurant, Tasha's book left in the back seat after a pointed look from Ms. Washington.

As they were walking toward the entrance, Tasha spotted Kim, waving to them. Today, she was wearing a pretty sundress with dogs doing the tango.

"Hey," John said, giving Kim a kiss. He took her hands in his and turned back to Ms. Washington and Tasha. "You remember Tasha from the library, right?"

Kim nodded. "She loves to read, just like me."

"Good to see you again, Kim," Ms. Washington said, even though her tone said she would rather still be at home. "Can we head inside? It might be suppertime, but it's still June."

They all shuffled into the restaurant. John was trying his best to talk up Kim, telling his mother about how hard it was for her to get time off since summer was the busiest wedding season. Ms. Washington was not impressed, and Tasha could tell Kim was a bit embarrassed.

She didn't understand why Ms. Washington was still mad at Kim. After all, it was John who had made plans and not followed through.

Tasha decided to ignore the awkwardness and be excited that the place was an all-you-can-eat home-style buffet. When she and her mom had the money to treat themselves, they always went to a similar restaurant and filled up on fried chicken and ice cream until they could barely move.

They were seated at a four-person table in the middle of the restaurant and once they were settled everyone went off to get their own food. John and Ms. Washington headed to the salad area, arguing in low voices, while Tasha moved toward the hot foods, and the pile of fried chicken on one end. Kim followed her.

"Did you find a good book the other day?" she asked with a smile. But as she handed a plate to Tasha, her smile faded. "Tasha, what's wrong?"

Tasha sniffled and shrugged, and Kim waited, giving her the time she needed to wade through her feelings. "I, uh, used to come to a place like this with my mom."

Kim's expression instantly collapsed. "I am so sorry. Losing someone you love is difficult, but having your entire life upended besides is, well . . . it can feel impossible. And I know it can be hard to talk about too." Kim sighed and looked like she wanted to say something more, but just shook her head instead. "What did you and your mom like best about the restaurant you used to go to?"

The lump in Tasha's throat made it hard to get words out. "We, uh, used to start with dessert. But just a little bit, so we wouldn't ruin our appetite."

Kim smiled. "That's a good idea. Let's do that."

They each went to the dessert area of the buffet and picked out something small—a tiny piece of cherry cobbler for Kim, a small corner of chocolate cake for Tasha—before heading back to the table.

When they sat down, John's eyebrows jumped up. "Dessert? Are you skipping dinner?"

"Tasha's mom used to do dessert first, so I'm trying

something new," Kim said, beaming. "It's a great idea, honestly."

Ms. Washington pushed her salad plate to the side. "You know, that is a great idea. I'm going to go get a dish of ice cream. John?"

John nodded and followed Ms. Washington as she led the way to the dessert area. They each came back with a small dish, and when Kim caught Tasha's eye, she winked. Tasha didn't know why, but the moment made her feel better.

The rest of the meal went without incident. Tasha ate as many fried chicken legs as she could, along with fried okra and lots of mashed potatoes and gravy. She even ate a plate full of green beans after Ms. Washington raised an eyebrow at her lack of vegetables and said in a low voice, "I don't see anything green on that plate." Tasha could've argued that the fried okra were technically green under the cornmeal, but she already knew that no one talked back to Ms. Washington.

By the time they left, Tasha was full and sleepy, and Kim was chatting happily with Ms. Washington, who had thawed enough to at least muster responses to the younger woman's questions.

John watched Kim's car pull away before they got back into his car. They'd barely left the parking lot before he was turned around in his seat grinning at Tasha. "So, what do you think?"

"I think you'd best keep your eyes on the road," Ms. Washington said, and John turned back to his driving while Tasha wondered why John was so eager to know how she felt about Kim.

Not that it mattered. Kim seemed nice. And Tasha had spent about as much time with her as she had her father. She wasn't sure why that bothered her, but it did.

The rest of the trip back to the trailer passed in silence, and by the time they pulled into the trailer park John was whistling happily to himself while Ms. Washington gave him a worried look.

It wasn't until Tasha had brushed her teeth and made her way to bed that she wondered if John was planning on trying to make Kim her new mom.

And she wasn't quite sure how she felt about that either.

9

Tasha finished all the books she'd checked out before she decided that she was probably going to have to find Ellie and apologize for how she acted in the library. The memory of their conversation made her feel awful, and the more she tried not to think about it, the worse she felt. Every time Tasha went to town with Ms. Washington they would drive by Ellie's place, and when Ellie was outside, Tasha could feel her staring at the car, at her. Ms. Washington would give her a wave and a smile and say, "Do you know Ellie? You should go say hi. She's a good kid."

Tasha knew that Ellie was a good kid—she shared her Popsicles, after all—and even though she really didn't want to talk anymore about murder ghosts or decomposing cats, Tasha decided that she had to be mature about this. And so one morning after eating a bowl of Fruity O's, she got ready to face the consequences of her actions.

"Ms. Washington, is it okay if I go for a walk?"

"Of course, child," Ms. Washington said. She sat in her favorite chair, watching a TV trial about a security deposit, whatever that was. "Be careful of the cars in the road."

Tasha walked toward the playground, hoping Ellie was somewhere, anywhere else today. But the girl was outside of her trailer, watering her tomatoes where they baked in the sun. They were twice as big as the last time Tasha saw them.

"Hi," Tasha said awkwardly.

Ellie's attention stayed on the watering can she held. "Hey," she said. "We don't have any more Popsicles."

Tasha swallowed hard. She wasn't great at making friends. She could always feel the moment where she said the wrong thing or did the wrong thing and other kids would lose interest. But even if she and Ellie couldn't be friends, she didn't want Ellie to think she was a jerk.

"I didn't come for a Popsicle. I came to say I'm sorry. I was rude to you in the library. I shouldn't have been like that."

If Ellie was surprised at the apology, she didn't show it. She stood up straight, the water in the can sloshing a bit. "Okay. Thanks. What do you want?"

Tasha shook her head. "That was it, just wanted to say I'm sorry."

Ellie shifted her weight from one foot to the other. "Oh, okay."

"Did you, uh, want some help?" Tasha asked, gesturing to the plants.

"Yeah, if you want."

So Tasha picked up an extra watering can and helped Ellie soak each of the plants so they'd make it through the heat of the day. It was hard work, and Ellie spent most of the time bossing Tasha around. Which was fine. She kind of deserved it after being so mean.

When they'd soaked every pot until water ran out the bottom, Ellie finally smiled. "Thanks. That was much easier with you helping. Want a Fudgsicle?"

Tasha smiled. "I thought you didn't have any Popsicles?"

"Fudgsicles are chocolate flavored, so not a Popsicle." Ellie disappeared around the back of the trailer and reappeared soon after. "We have a freezer on the back porch," she said in response to Tasha's confused look.

They settled onto the steps to Ellie's trailer and ate their Fudgsicles. Tasha was almost done with hers when her curiosity got the better of her. "Where did you learn so much about ghosts?"

"There used to be a kid who lived here. Franklin. He was really smart, and he told me how there was a murder ghost that lived in the marsh. He said if you see blinking lights out across the water at night, it's the murder ghost looking for a victim. He said you can tell a murder ghost because of the long hair, wet smell, and the way they move, that kind of jerk they have."

Tasha licked the last of her Fudgsicle from the stick and frowned. She remembered something in the book she had read about lights on the water, but nothing like the ghost Ellie described. She wanted to have an answer for Ellie, something that would help her move on from the whole murder ghost nonsense. "Are you sure he wasn't just trying to scare you? In one of the apartment complexes I lived in, there were a couple of older boys who told me and some other kids that if you looked in a mirror and said 'Candyman' three times, a man covered in bees would come to kill you. I was terrified to go into the bathroom by myself until my mom explained it was the plot of a movie.

Maybe Franklin was just talking about a TV show or something that he saw?"

"Yeah, I thought that as well. But a lot of old people have died over the past few months. Harold wasn't the first, you know, and—"

"Yeah, Ms. Washington told me," Tasha said. "It's sad, but that's what happens with old people, right?"

Ellie sighed, clearly frustrated. "Look, we don't have to talk about this."

Tasha couldn't quite hide her surprise. "No?"

"No. Because you don't believe and, well . . . I'd rather just hang out with you from now on, and not talk about this. If that's okay."

Tasha smiled, feeling much better than she had when she'd decided to walk down to Ellie's trailer. "It is. And, uh, cool."

Ellie said then that she had to do her chores, so Tasha made her way back to Ms. Washington's trailer to spend the rest of the afternoon in the air-conditioning. Before she got back, though, a voice called out to her.

"You, there. Child! Can you help me out?"

Tasha looked around until she spotted a small old white woman standing on a porch of a gray-and-white trailer. It took a moment for Tasha to recognize that she was Ms. Greta.

"Sure, Ms. Greta. How are you doing?"

The woman narrowed her eyes, like she didn't know how Tasha knew her name, but she didn't say anything about it. "You wouldn't happen to have seen my dog around here anywhere, have you? Small guy, answers to Fredo."

Tasha shook her head. "When was the last time you saw him?"

Ms. Greta didn't answer right away. The old woman's eyes were slightly unfocused, and Tasha shifted uncomfortably. She knew that sometimes old people got confused.

"Well, I suppose he'll come home when he's ready," Ms. Greta finally said. She pulled an envelope from the pocket of her bathrobe and waved it at Tasha. "Would you be a dear and drop this in the mailbox as you go past the office?"

The park office was in the middle of the row of trailers, not that far away. Tasha nodded, and Ms. Greta extended the envelope toward her. As she did, her robe fell back to reveal strange marks on her arm. The skin looked rubbed raw, and the red marks glowed angrily, seeping with a strange liquid that made the injuries look wet and painful.

Tasha swallowed dryly and thought once more of

Old Harold's hand and its missing skin. "Um, are you okay, Ms. Greta?" Tasha said.

"What?" The woman followed Tasha's gaze to her arms, as though seeing them for the first time. "Oh! I must've bumped into something. I've been sleeping terribly the past few nights. But I'm fine, child. Thank you for being so helpful."

Tasha took the letter carefully. The old lady waved at her then, and Tasha waved back, walking the letter to the nearby mailbox while the old woman stood on her porch and watched.

After, as Tasha walked home, she wondered if Ms. Greta had caught the same disease that Old Harold had. Tasha had read a lot about diseases on the internet and knew that there were illnesses like leprosy, which could cause body parts to rot off a person. And this was the second time that the old woman had talked about not sleeping well.

Whatever it was, Tasha knew she had to tell her grandma. Sick or no, Ms. Greta looked like she needed help, and sometimes Tasha wondered that if her mom had gotten help sooner, she would've been okay. They had to make sure Ms. Greta was all right.

Ellie's warning about the thing in the marsh arose in Tasha's mind unbidden, and she dismissed the thought. Old people got sick. Even young people got sick. That didn't mean a ghost was behind it.

Ellie was right about one thing, though. It was nice to have someone to talk to.

10

Cool air washed over Tasha as she entered the trailer. It was such a relief that she sighed. It was bright outside, much brighter than inside Ms. Washington's house, so it took a moment for Tasha's eyes to adjust and for her to realize that they had company.

"Tasha! There you are. Come and say hello to Kim."

It had been more than a week since they'd all gone to eat together, and Tasha had not seen Kim since. They'd gone back to the library so that Tasha could get more books in the dragon series she was reading, but Kim hadn't been there, and Tasha had been a little disappointed. She wasn't sure how she felt about Kim and John being together, but Kim liked Tasha's dad and seemed to like her as well. Something that felt even more true when Tasha saw the wide smile Kim wore as Tasha took off her shoes.

"I stopped by because I was wondering if you wanted to spend the day with me. I have the day off and I was going to head over to the fabric store. I thought maybe you'd like to ride along."

Tasha looked from her grandmother to Kim, trying to figure out whose idea it was for her to spend a day with her father's girlfriend. But neither Ms. Washington nor Kim gave anything away, so Tasha shrugged. "Sure, okay."

"You don't have to if you don't want to," Kim said, climbing to her feet, her car keys already in her hand. "But I'd love some company, and your grandma said you might like to take a ride into town."

Ms. Washington nodded. "You two should spend some time together."

Kim smiled. "If you'd like we can grab some lunch on the way."

Tasha nodded before sending one last glance at her grandmother, wondering if the older woman had changed her opinion about Kim.

And then Tasha was heading back outside and into town.

Kim was excited about everything.

That was Tasha's thought when they entered the

87

fabric store. At the fast-food restaurant they'd visited—a burger place with about a million different toppings—Kim couldn't decide what she wanted most, finally just ordering the same thing as Tasha after the woman behind the register began to lose her patience. It was no different in the fabric store. Kim went from one fabric to the next, asking Tasha's opinion on each. Tasha didn't expect to have fun, and she still wasn't sure how she felt about Kim, but by the time Kim was waving down one of the ladies at the store to cut a bolt of fabric, Tasha had to admit that she was having a pretty good time.

"Don't you love these fun little whales?" the clerk said as she unrolled a cardboard spindle of fabric with little whales riding bicycles printed on it. It was silly and Tasha loved it.

"Yes! We couldn't resist," Kim said with a grin.

The lady from the store smiled at Tasha. "Your momma has good taste," she said.

Tasha found her tongue glued to the roof of her mouth. She wanted to make sure the woman knew that Kim wasn't her mom, that she barely knew her. But Kim didn't say anything, and Tasha found that she couldn't find the words before the moment had passed. So Tasha just smiled awkwardly.

Later, when they were driving back to Ms. Washington's house, Kim cleared her throat. "I'm sorry that I didn't immediately correct the lady at the fabric store," she said. "I didn't think it really made a difference, but then I realized it probably did—to you. I can imagine it was a little uncomfortable for the person at the store to bring that up. Especially since I know that you and your dad haven't hung out all that much."

Tasha couldn't help the sudden scowl on her face, and Kim noticed, patting Tasha's arm. "I'm sorry your dad has been so busy. He's been working so much lately, and when he has some time off, he likes to go out with his friends. Heck, sometimes I don't even see him until the morning because he'll stay out all night."

Kim grew quiet then, and Tasha didn't know what to say. She'd figured that John was spending all his time with Kim, but apparently he'd been ditching her as well.

But when Kim spoke, she wasn't thinking of herself. "It's not okay that he hasn't spent more time with you. I'd really like to help fix that. But I'm also sorry if I overstepped in any way, especially when I didn't correct that lady about being your mom. I will next time if you want me to. I suppose that . . ." Kim shook her head.

"What?" Tasha asked.

Kim hesitated, but only for a moment. "I guess I just didn't want you to think that I hated the idea."

Tasha nodded. "It's okay. It was just awkward and I didn't want to say anything."

Kim's eyes flicked between the road and Tasha. "So we're good?"

"Yeah, we're good."

"Good. Because next time I get paid we are definitely going back to get that fabric with the octopus reading books," she said.

For the first time in as long as she could remember, Tasha laughed. Maybe because it sounded like something her mom would've said.

Before she knew it, they were turning into the entrance to the trailer park. Kim pulled up in front of Ms. Washington's trailer and let Tasha out with a smile.

"I'm sorry your dad couldn't join us. I know he'll be sad he missed our super-awesome hang."

Tasha shrugged. She wasn't so sure that was true. "It's okay. I had fun."

She got out of Kim's car and waved as she pulled off, then climbed the steps back into Ms. Washington's trailer.

Her grandmother was still right where she'd left her, and she peered at Tasha as she entered. "So, how was it?" she asked.

"Fun," Tasha said.

"How do you feel about making some cookies before dinner? We could make snickerdoodles or maybe sugar cookies. Which do you prefer?"

"Sugar cookies," Tasha said, following Ms. Washington as she stood and headed into the kitchen. The older woman began to look through cupboards, laying out the ingredients on the counter while Tasha sat at the kitchen table, trying to stay out of the way.

Tasha watched her quietly for a minute. "Ms. Washington, have you talked to Ms. Greta recently?"

Ms. Washington pulled a mixer out of the cupboard and frowned. "Now that you mention it, I haven't seen her this week. Why?"

Tasha chewed on the inside of her cheek. "I saw her earlier today, before I went out with Kim. She seemed . . . confused." Tasha didn't know how to tell Ms. Washington that Ms. Greta hadn't seemed to recognize her, so she said, "She couldn't find her dog. Alfredo?"

"*Fredo*. It's a character from an old movie. And that's too bad. She adores that dog. Do you remember him? She had him last time she stopped by."

Tasha nodded. "I remember."

"I wonder when he went missing. We could go out and look for him."

Tasha frowned. "She didn't seem too worried."

At that, Ms. Washington turned to look at Tasha. "What makes you say that?"

Tasha shrugged. "She said, 'He'll turn up' or something like that."

Ms. Washington looked out the window, in the direction of Ms. Greta's trailer.

In that moment, Tasha remembered one of the old ladies in the apartments they'd lived in when she was in fourth grade. The woman had fallen and hit her head, and no one found her until it was too late. Her mom had said it was unfortunate that people always threw the elderly away, ignoring them when they need help the most. What if something had happened to Ms. Greta and it was causing her to behave strangely?

"Maybe we should go check on her," Tasha said, "just to make sure she's okay."

Ms. Washington nodded in agreement. "That's a good idea. I'll call the front office and see if they can have someone go by her house right now and check on her." Ms. Washington paused and gave Tasha a very serious look. "If you notice anything else strange, you tell me, okay? There are lots of older folks in this park, and they need us to take care of them."

Tasha couldn't help but notice that Ms. Washington did not seem to count herself as one of the older people in the park. But she kept that observation to herself.

She was having a good day. She didn't want to ruin it.

11

After a dinner of the best pork chops Tasha had ever tasted, Ms. Washington wrapped up a few sugar cookies and handed them to Tasha.

"The office said that they checked on Ms. Greta and she was doing fine, but I tried calling her and she's not answering. Perhaps you could run these over to her and see how she's feeling?"

Tasha took the cookies with a nod and ran out of the front door into the summer evening.

The sun had already dipped beyond the horizon, and the streetlights on the main road cast a feeble glow. Some of the lights were burned out, and the deep shadows between the trailers made Tasha uneasy. Wandering around all by herself, Tasha could understand how Ellie could come to think she'd seen something frightening slinking in the darkness. She said the ghost had long stringy hair and smelled bad; the Spanish moss hanging from a nearby tree looked just like that, and Tasha could smell the stinky stagnant water from the marsh on the evening air.

The scent reminded Tasha of the time the kitchen sink in an apartment where she and her mom were living got clogged, and they had to wait for the landlord to clear the drain. It had taken two whole days for him to show up, and the water in the pipes had taken on a sour, noxious smell. It was so bad that Tasha's mom had called the man and yelled, threatening not to pay rent if it wasn't fixed. Tasha couldn't remember much else about the incident, but she remembered the plumber taking the sink apart and a stench like moldy death filling the apartment.

The closer Tasha got to Ms. Greta's trailer, the more it began to smell like something spoiled, and the damp, fetid smell had Tasha holding her arm to her nose as she walked. But it wasn't enough, and by the time she began to climb the steps to Ms. Greta's porch, Tasha was gagging, afraid she was going to be sick.

There was something very wrong at Ms. Greta's house. Maybe *her* sink had gotten clogged. Tasha knocked once and then again, and when no one answered the door, she just set the cookies down. The smell was too bad to wait for the old woman to answer.

Tasha had no sooner stepped off the porch than she saw a flicker of movement from the corner of her eye. She froze, terror sending a chill over her skin. Because even though she wasn't looking right at the shape that was looming in the shadow beside Ms. Greta's trailer, she could feel the wrongness of it. Her arm was still held across her face, and she lowered it slowly. The smell was overpowering, dead fish and rotting vegetation, and a deep rot that belonged not to a marsh but to a grave.

Tasha didn't want to look. But she couldn't help herself. It was as though she was compelled to turn her head, to spare a glance at that dark space between the trailers where the streetlights didn't quite reach.

So Tasha didn't fight the unbearable urge. She looked.

For a couple of heartbeats, she felt embarrassed relief. There was nothing there; she'd just let Ellie's panic and silliness infect her.

But then the shadow lurched.

Tasha was unable to move, to speak, to flee. All she could do was watch.

The thing—it looked almost too solid to be a ghost—was tall and skinny, taller and skinnier than any person should be. It was all jutting angles and grasping hands. Long stringy hair hung down to its knees, and its arms were freakishly long. It looked naked, but there was nothing human about the body, which glistened wetly in the scant streetlight. Tasha couldn't quite make out what kind of liquid was on the thing, but it was dark in color. But the worst part was the sound it made as it contemplated Tasha: a gasping croak that was not quite animal, but far from human. *And the smell.* It seemed to grow stronger the longer Tasha looked at the thing.

It was Tasha's gagging that finally broke the spell. She was going to be sick. But she couldn't be—not where that thing could get her.

The nausea cut through her fear, and she was able to start moving, her flip-flops making a slapping sound as she ran, breathless, back in the direction she'd come from. A sob hitched in her throat, and she pumped her arms harder, ignoring the painful stitch that bloomed in her side.

When she arrived at Ms. Washington's trailer, Tasha slammed inside and ran right to her room. She closed the door behind her and dove under the covers, trying to get warm. She began to shake, her breaths ragged gasps. She tried to come up with some explanation for what she'd seen, but it was impossible. The thing had been as tall and narrow as a small tree, but no tree could have tricked Tasha into seeing what she saw; there wasn't even a tree near Ms. Greta's trailer. And the smell—

Tasha would never forget that smell.

A moment later, Ms. Washington was knocking on the door.

"Tasha? What's the matter, baby?"

Tasha hesitated, but only for a second. "Nothing, Ms. Washington," she called out. She knew how she'd reacted when Ellie had told her about the murder ghost. There was no way she could tell Ms. Washington what she'd seen. She'd just think Tasha had been reading too many of her books. "I, uh, my stomach just doesn't feel very good."

"Did you try pooping?" said Ms. Washington.

Somehow, the old lady talking about poop burned away Tasha's fear in a way that nothing else could. The embarrassment almost made her wish she was back outside facing down the murder ghost again. Almost.

"Uh, no," Tasha finally replied.

"Okay, give it a try. If that doesn't work, let me know and I'll get you some ginger ale."

Ms. Washington walked away and Tasha lay in bed. She didn't have to use the bathroom, which was lucky, as she was reasonably sure that she was never leaving her room again.

12

Tasha woke the next morning feeling no better than she had the night before. She'd slept terribly, waking what felt like every few minutes in a panic, certain there was someone—or something—in her room.

But each time she'd been alone.

When daylight had finally begun to creep between her blinds, she conceded defeat and hauled herself out of bed. There was something she had to do.

Last night she had been too scared to think about *A Guide to Southern Myths and Legends*. Tasha hadn't found anything like what Ellie had described in the section about ghosts, the one entitled "Haints and Haunts of the South." But now that Tasha had seen the creature for herself, she wondered if there might be some information in another section: "Witches and Supernatural Oddities." Tasha was convinced there was something she'd read about that looked like the sinewy, stooped thing she'd seen near Ms. Greta's trailer. She needed to get the book and double-check.

It was earlier than Tasha was usually awake, and for the first time, she emerged from her room to see her father. He and Ms. Washington were in the kitchen, arguing in low voices.

"What Tasha needs is her father, not yet another person you can leave her with while—" Tasha heard before she closed her bedroom door and Ms. Washington hushed. "Tasha? That you?" she called.

"Yes'm," Tasha said, slinking out of her bedroom. Ms. Washington was at the stove, making bacon, while John sat at the kitchen table drinking a soda. Tasha wasn't sure where to be, so she just sort of leaned against the wall of the hallway awkwardly, somewhat in the kitchen but also not.

"We didn't wake you, did we?" John asked, all smiles. There was something so strange about seeing her father in Ms. Washington's house that Tasha just stared at him for a moment as she tried to think of a proper response.

"No, I didn't sleep very well," she finally said.

"Well, I'm glad you're awake, because I have news."

Tasha looked from John to Ms. Washington, who

didn't appear nearly as excited about whatever the news was as he did.

"Kim and I are getting *married*," John said.

"Oh," Tasha said. "Congratulations."

John's smile faded as he looked from Ms. Washington to Tasha and back. "Not you too."

Tasha frowned. "Not me too, what?"

"Your daddy seems to think people should enjoy getting life-altering news first thing in the morning," Ms. Washington said.

A pained look flitted across John's face before he found his smile again. "You always say you want to know what's going on in my life the moment it happens," he said to his mother. "I proposed late last night, and, well, here I am." He finished his soda and crushed the can.

"But marriage? I just met the girl. Not to mention Tasha has only just met you, has just come to live in a strange new place—"

"Eh, she's fine, right, kiddo?" John asked.

The last place Tasha wanted to be was in the middle of this fight. "I have to go to the bathroom," she said, deciding that she could grab *A Guide to Southern Myths and Legends* later.

She closed the toilet lid and sat down, reading old copies of *Reader's Digest* until she heard the front door slam, John heading back to wherever it was he spent his time. Kim's house, probably. They were engaged, after all.

When Tasha came back out Ms. Washington was placing bacon on a plate. Tasha wasn't sure, but it looked like she might have been crying.

She gave Tasha a smile when she reappeared. "Pancakes or waffles?"

"Waffles," Tasha said, and Ms. Washington pulled out a waffle iron. Nothing else was said about John or his impending wedding.

And that was fine by Tasha.

After Ms. Washington's regular daytime TV shows began, Tasha went outside to find Ellie, the book of southern legends and monsters tucked under her arm. While she would've liked the incident from the night before to be like John's engagement—its reality acknowledged and then put to the side, never to be discussed again—there was no setting aside the vision of a soaking-wet thing with too-long hair. And when she'd finally managed to get to the book after breakfast and turned to the section about witches, the drawings she found there confirmed what Ellie had been saying all along:

There was something terrifying haunting Shady Pines Estates.

Ellie wasn't outside when Tasha arrived at her trailer, so she waited in front for a little while before finally steeling her nerve and knocking on the front door. No one answered, and while Tasha was considering whether or not to knock again, the sound of running footsteps came from inside. The door popped open, and there was Ellie, her hair mussed like she'd just woken up. She wore a nightgown that was far too short, like it was meant for a much younger girl, covered in bright pink unicorns and purple ice-cream cones.

"Hey. What time is it?" Ellie asked.

"I saw it," Tasha said, unable to keep everything from bursting out.

"Saw what?"

"The murder ghost. But it's not a ghost at all! It's something else. It was just like you said. There was this smell, and I almost barfed, and then there was—"

"Whoa, whoa! Hold on. I have to put on real clothes." Ellie closed the door and then reappeared, no longer wearing pajamas but her hair still a mess. She held the door open and gestured for Tasha to come in.

Tasha entered into a dark, messy trailer. Food wrappers covered a battered coffee table, and a cat was kneading at a ratty pillow in the corner, giving Tasha what felt like a dirty look. The smell of old fried food and stale cigarettes clung to everything.

"My aunt isn't here right now, so I'm supposed to stay inside," Ellie said, flinging herself onto the couch. A blanket with a howling wolf and a rainbow was tossed carelessly on one end, and Tasha moved it to the side as she sat down. "Are you hungry?"

Tasha shook her head and Ellie leaned forward and snagged a mostly empty bag of sour-cream-and-onion chips from the table. She crammed a handful in her mouth, chewing fast and swallowing. "Tell me exactly what happened."

Tasha recounted the events from the night before. Once she began describing the misshapen creature, Ellie stopped eating and just stared at Tasha with her mouth hanging open.

"That's exactly what I saw," Ellie said, crumpling up the bag and throwing it back on the coffee table. "I think we need to investigate."

Tasha blinked. "What? No, we need to figure out

how to protect ourselves and everyone else against it. That's why I brought this." She held up Ms. Washington's copy of *A Guide to Southern Myths and Legends*. "When I saw the thing, I remembered something I'd read in here. It's not in the section about ghosts at all."

Ellie shook her head. "Wait, so I *didn't* see a ghost?"

"Look at this." Tasha flipped through the pages until she came to a rough drawing of a creature with long wet hair and claws. The thing was misshapen, the arms and fingers too long and disproportionate. The face was completely hidden by the long stringy hair. It didn't look exactly like what Tasha had seen, but it was the creature's skin that gave it away—or its lack thereof. The thing was covered in blood and muscle, as if its skin had been peeled off. It was wet and slender and inhuman—just like the thing last night.

"That's sort of what I saw. It was dark, though," Ellie said. "And I was scared."

"Me too. It wasn't until I woke up this morning that I remembered there had been something similar in the book. It's a *boo hag*."

"A boo hag?" Ellie said as Tasha handed her the book.

"Yup. Apparently, a boo hag is a regular person

who made a deal with a witch so that they could live forever. The witch makes them immortal, but takes their soul in return, so the boo hag needs to draw the life out of other people to survive. They still look like a normal person—until it's time for them to go hunting. Then, they take off their skin." Tasha couldn't help the little shiver that ran down her spine. "A boo hag can take days or even weeks to kill a person, slowly sucking out their victim's soul bit by bit. I think this is what killed Mr. Harold."

Ellie looked back at the book, and Tasha waited for her to finish reading the full description. When Ellie looked up her eyes were wide. "It says here that a boo hag 'rides' people? Like they're a horse? How does that even work?"

Tasha shook her head. "I'm not sure, but a lot of the other things we know are true." She pointed to each passage in the book as she made her points. "Smells like rotting fish or icky water. Has long stringy hair. Has extra-long fingers to hold on to its victims. It also says they drain the life force of their victims by sucking out their breath at night while they're sleeping—causing nightmares, making them tired and languid, and leaving marks on their skin." She looked Ellie dead in the eye. "Ms. Greta said she hasn't been sleeping well for over a week, and the last time I talked to her she had weird marks on her arms. I thought maybe she was sick or something."

Ellie frowned. "Do you think the boo hag is feeding on Ms. Greta?" she asked.

"I don't know," said Tasha. "Maybe we should talk to her, see if we can find out?"

"It says here that a boo hag can only be defeated by the sun—if it rises before they're able to get back into their skin, they're doomed to live skinless forever. Sort of like a vampire, I guess," Ellie said. "There's a whole lot about skins here. Do you think the boo hag takes the skins of the people they kill as well?"

Tasha told Ellie again about the skinless arm she saw under the sheet outside Old Harold's trailer. "Maybe the boo hag has to make a new skin, just in case its old one wears out or gets taken," she wondered aloud. "It says in there that they can get into someone's house through the tiniest crack or hole, and they form connections with people quickly. There is even a story about a lady who proposed marriage to a man a week after meeting him, only for the man to discover, on their wedding night, that she was a boo hag—and she tried to skin him!"

Ellie suddenly jumped to her feet, startling Tasha.

The book fell to the floor and Tasha leaned over to pick it up.

"There's only one way to save Ms. Greta," Ellie said, her expression grim. "We need to figure out who the boo hag is and stop them."

"How are we supposed to do that?" Tasha asked, and Ellie pointed to the door.

"We start by visiting the place the boo hag was last seen. Maybe there's a clue as to the monster's real identity. Mr. Harold wasn't the first person who seemed healthy one day and the next week he was dead—it's been happening for a few months now. I'm thinking it must be someone who lives in the trailer park."

Tasha wasn't so sure—the boo hag could be from anywhere; it might just come here to hunt—but Ellie was already bounding out of the trailer.

Tasha wasn't so sure she wanted to solve the mystery of the boo hag. If it were up to her, she'd never see that thing ever again. She'd convince Ms. Washington to pack their bags, get the heck out of Shady Pines Estates, and never look back. Just leave the boo hag, the dead people, and her deadbeat dad behind.

But then she remembered what her mom had told her:

It's not the things in the dark that scare us—it's the

darkness itself. We're most frightened of what we don't know. That's why we face our fears, Tash. Then we won't be afraid anymore.

Tasha's mom had been talking about some silly scary movie. But remembering it now, she knew she couldn't let Ellie hunt a monster by herself.

She took a deep breath and ran after Ellie toward Ms. Greta's house.

13

Even though the sun was burning bright in the sky, Tasha couldn't help but feel a chill as she and Ellie strode toward Ms. Greta's trailer. Things weren't supposed to be scary in the daylight, but Tasha walked with a heavy weight of dread in her middle. What would they do if they found a real clue that the boo hag had been there? Tasha imagined finding a lock of stringy hair or some of the thing's blood. She was walking so slowly now that Ellie stopped and looked over her shoulder.

"What's wrong?" she asked.

"I just . . ." She couldn't finish the sentence.

Ellie walked back and put her arm around Tasha, urging her forward gently while also giving a measure of comfort. "When I saw the thing, I couldn't eat for like a whole day. Every time I thought about that smell, and the way it looked, I just got . . ." Ellie shuddered, part exaggeration, but also part truth. "I'm not as scared now because you're with me. We need to check on Ms. Greta, right? And if things go wrong later, and the boo hag appears, we can fight it off. I just know it. We can be strong together."

Tasha forced a smile. A monster that skinned people could easily handle the two of them. But if Ellie could be brave, she could too. And besides, Ellie was right. They had to help Ms. Greta. If they didn't, she'd likely end up like Old Harold. They nodded and continued on.

Ellie pressed her back up against the front of Ms. Greta's trailer, right next to the steps to the porch. While most of the trailers had steps on the side of the house, Ms. Greta's were in the front facing the street. Ellie gestured for Tasha to stand next to her, so she hurried over and did just that.

"Okay, on the count of three?" Ellie whispered.

Tasha nodded. She couldn't speak. It felt as though her throat had closed up. What would they do if they found another dead cat? Or even worse, a dead person?

"One . . ."

Tasha shifted her weight slightly and wiped her sweaty palms on the legs of her shorts.

"Two . . ."

She leaned forward slightly and prepared to move. She knew this was a stupid idea, but they had to do *something*.

"Three!"

Both of the girls leapt into the space between the trailers, facing down the long side yard where Tasha had seen the boo hag—and immediately screamed as they saw a humanlike shape hunched in the shade.

"What the—! Tasha, what are you doing?"

John was in the space between the trailers, on his hands and knees in the short grass.

"You girls scared the crap out of me," he said, angrily climbing to his feet.

Ellie's eyes were wide as saucers and she seemed to have lost the ability to speak, so it was left to Tasha. "We were, ah, playing hide-and-seek. We thought you were someone else." The lie sounded silly, even to her own ears.

But John just sighed. "Well, you shouldn't go around scaring people like that. It's rude."

"*Well*, what are you doing sneaking around next to Ms. Greta's trailer?" Tasha asked, turning John's indignation back around on him.

"I'm looking for her stupid dog," he said. "Your

113

grandmother said Fredo is missing and asked me to see if maybe he was stuck under the trailer or something. So I was looking through the gap in the skirting." He pointed to a space where the sheet metal that hid the wheels under Ms. Greta's house had been bent back, offering the perfect opening for a cat or small dog to creep through.

"How can you see under the trailer without a flashlight?" Ellie asked, finally finding her voice.

"I can't, which is why I'm going to go back and find one. Tasha, you head home once you guys are done with your game, okay? We need to have a chat."

John walked past them, his shoulders tight with annoyance. Tasha watched him go, her fear replaced with anger. She didn't like how John had talked to her. He had no interest in being a proper parent, but now he wanted to tell her what to do? Please.

Once he was out of earshot, Ellie nudged Tasha. "That's your dad?"

Tasha nodded slowly. "Yep."

"Are you in trouble?"

"No. Maybe. I don't know him that well so I can't really tell." Tasha shrugged. "But I should probably get going."

Ellie nodded. "Yeah. He looked kind of upset." She

opened her mouth to say something and then snapped it shut, frowning as her gaze landed on something in the grass. "Hey. Do you see that?"

"What?"

"Over there. What is that?"

Ellie walked farther into the grass, right where John had been crawling around. She nudged something with the toe of her flip-flop and her eyes widened.

Tasha ran over and looked to where Ellie was staring. There in the grass, shining wetly in the hot sun, was a silvery piece of . . . something. It looked like fish skin, and maybe a little bit of pond scum.

Tasha stared at the silvery skin and wet algae and swallowed dryly. "How did this even get here?"

"I don't know, but it's weird, right?"

"Very," Tasha reluctantly agreed. "We should check on Ms. Greta."

They headed back to the stairs and climbed them. The cookies Tasha had left the night before were gone, but no amount of knocking on the front door was met with a response. The trailer was quiet, no sound of footsteps of someone inside.

"Do you think she's . . . ?" Ellie began.

"She might be resting," Tasha said, not wanting to think about what Ellie was suggesting. "If my dad was looking for her dog, maybe that means she talked to my grandma today. I'll go home and find out."

After bidding Ellie farewell, Tasha made her slow way back to the trailer. She had a feeling there was going to be trouble waiting for her, but if she could face her fears about the boo hag, then she could face down anything.

At least, she hoped.

When Tasha got home, Ms. Washington and John were at the kitchen table waiting for her. Ms. Washington looked like she'd accidentally bitten into a lemon, but John's earlier anger was gone, replaced by one of his usual smiles.

"Tasha! There you are," he said, pulling out one of the chairs. "We have something important to tell you."

She sat down and John took a deep breath.

"So, like I told you earlier this morning, Kim and I are getting married. But there's more."

Tasha didn't say anything. She still didn't know what to think about the whole thing. Didn't people spend a lot of time together before they got married? Tasha had thought that Kim and her dad had just started dating, mostly from the way Ms. Washington still talked to Kim like she was a stranger.

"After Kim and I get married," he continued, "you're going to move in with us."

Tasha blinked once, and then again. "*You* want me to move in with you?"

"Of course. This is the perfect opportunity for us to get to know each other better, and Kim has space in her house." John asked, "Aren't you excited?"

Tasha had no words, mostly because she wasn't quite sure how she felt. Not happy and not sad, exactly, but more annoyed that once again it felt like John was making a decision when it was convenient for him, and how anyone else felt—including Tasha—didn't really matter.

"What if I don't want to?" she asked.

Judging from the looks on both John's and Ms. Washington's faces, Tasha had just stepped right into the middle of their earlier argument.

"Told you it was too soon," Ms. Washington said. "The child has barely adjusted to her mother's passing and now you're springing a stepmother on her. Have you even asked your bride-to-be how she feels about this?"

"Are you kidding? This was Kim's idea!" He laughed nervously, and Tasha had the feeling that he was lying. Or at least exaggerating. "She had a great time the day you spent together."

Ms. Washington harrumphed and crossed her arms, and John stood.

"Well, Kim is making a big dinner to celebrate, and I wanted to tell you in person beforehand." John said it like it was all settled, which Tasha guessed it was, for him. "It has to be an early dinner because she has work to do, wedding season and all. Be by around six."

John stood, giving his mom a kiss on the cheek and giving Tasha an awkward pat before leaving, slamming the door a little harder than necessary on his way out.

"That boy . . . ," Ms. Washington muttered, swallowing whatever else she wanted to say. She stood there, hands on her hips, and sighed. "Well, I suppose you'd best take a shower before we head over. Your daddy brought by a dress Kim made for you, if you want to wear it."

Tasha nodded. She had a feeling she was in for a very eventful evening.

Sure enough, Tasha returned from her shower to find a new dress on her bed. It was sewn from the material Kim had said she was going to go back and buy at the fabric store: a print of an octopus reading a bunch of books, one in each tentacle. It fit perfectly, and for just a flash, she thought that no matter how bad her dad was at being a dad, at least Kim might be a pretty good mom.

Immediately she thought of her mom and felt guilty.

The drive to Kim's house was quiet, with both Ms. Washington and Tasha lost in their own thoughts. Kim lived in a house a few miles from the trailer park, down a dirt road with lots of trees pressing in, far away from the smell of the marsh. It was a nice house, with a huge flowering bush that nearly swallowed the front, and a fancy-looking lattice that surrounded one side of the house, turning a concrete patio into a cozy outdoor space, complete with a barbecue grill for cookouts. It was much too uncomfortable to sit outside, the day still humid and sweltering, but Tasha thought it would be nice to sit behind the lattice and the branches of the flowering bush and read a book when the weather was a bit cooler.

She wasn't sure why she thought that, and again felt a little guilty for it. She liked living with Ms. Washington. No matter what her son was, she was a good grandma. How would she feel if Tasha up and moved in with Kim and John?

Tasha reached out for Ms. Washington's hand as they walked up to the door, holding it like she was still a little kid. Ms. Washington didn't say anything. She just squeezed Tasha's hand with her own, as though she knew what Tasha was feeling, even if Tasha wasn't sure she knew herself.

And then Kim was opening the front door, her smile bright and welcoming, her brown hair down now and hanging over her shoulder, long and silky like a fairy-tale princess come to life.

"Hello! You're right on time."

She gestured for them all to enter, the cool air beckoning as well. John was nowhere to be seen.

"John's taking a shower," Kim said as if reading their minds, and closed the door behind them. "Can I get you some sweet tea, or a soda?"

"Sweet tea," Ms. Washington answered, and Tasha nodded in agreement.

"Great. I'll be right back."

Kim moved off into the back of the house, past a dining room. Tasha couldn't help but stare in awe. She'd never been anywhere so nice. It smelled like pork chops and sugar cookies in the house, making her stomach growl. The carpet was deep and plush, a dark blue, while the walls were a sedate cream. All the furniture looked new and extra comfy, the couch just begging to be sat upon. There were fancy pictures of mythological creatures framed on every wall: a unicorn drinking from a misty mountain lake, a dragon spitting fire at an erstwhile prince. There was no TV that Tasha could see.

Kim came back with the sweet teas. "How do you like the dress?"

Tasha smiled. "I like it a lot. Thanks." She still couldn't quite believe Kim had gone back to the fabric store and bought the material like she'd promised she would.

"I'm glad it fits! I had to guess your size. I even added pockets into the sides."

"You made that when you didn't even know Tasha's size?" Ms. Washington asked. Whether she was skeptical or impressed, Tasha couldn't tell.

"I sure did. I'm pretty good at guessing people's sizes," Kim said, and turned back to Tasha. "Hey, do you want to see my sewing room?"

No one had any objections, so they followed Kim down the hallway to a small room with a bay window that looked out over a well-maintained garden. The room was crowded with bins filled with fabric, buttons, and other bits and bobs that Tasha couldn't really name. There was a sewing machine off to one side on a table, the only clear surface in the entire room. A closet held a stack of dresses wrapped in plastic and garment bags; from the look of them they were wedding and bridesmaid dresses. Very fancy.

"I'm working on a few things from home right now because I'm so behind at work, but I made you an apron, Mary, if you would like it?"

Ms. Washington looked at the apron Kim held out. There was a pattern of T-bone steaks on it, which Tasha thought was funny but she could tell Ms. Washington thought was ghastly.

"Well, thank you," she said with a tight smile. "This is something."

Kim turned back to Tasha with an eager expression. "Let me know if you like any of the other fabrics I have. If you do, I'd be happy to make you another dress."

Something warm welled up in Tasha, and she smiled. "Thanks. That's very nice."

Just then, John's voice came from the dining room. "Are we eating soon? I'm hungry."

Kim straightened. "Oh, I almost forgot the rolls. Let me grab them before they burn."

A minute later, they were all at the dining room

table—an actual dining room table and not a card table on the edge of the kitchen, like Tasha and her mom had so often used. Kim brought out plate after plate of food: There was chicken-fried steak and mashed potatoes, brown gravy and green beans, and even a basket of perfectly baked rolls and real butter. Every single time a new plate appeared, Ms. Washington's scowl deepened, so by the time the entire meal was ready to be served, she had a very stormy look indeed.

"Ma," John said when Kim went back to the kitchen to grab plates. "Don't be like that."

Ms. Washington smoothed her expression back to a more pleasant one, and Tasha wondered for the first time just how her own mom had gotten on with Ms. Washington. Had the old lady scowled at her like she was now scowling at Kim? Would Ms. Washington be mad at her if she liked Kim just as much as her grandmother? For some reason, the thought made Tasha feel sad, and by the time they were finished saying grace she was hard-pressed to eat much of the delicious food Kim had spooned onto her plate.

"So, Tasha, are you excited for school to start?" Kim asked as she took a helping of mashed potatoes.

"Not really," Tasha said, deciding to shove a mouthful of food in just so she could avoid the conversation.

She hated starting a new school, and this time she wouldn't even have her mom to make her lunch every day and slip in a note telling her that she was doing good.

"John still has to get her enrolled," Ms. Washington said, as though she sensed Tasha's discomfort. "He's been a bit distracted."

"I suppose that's my fault," Kim said with an awkward laugh, cutting into a piece of meat.

John waved the comment aside. "Once we're married Kim can make sure Tasha has what she needs."

"Speaking of which, when are y'all getting married?" Ms. Washington asked, her tone sweet. Tasha noticed that Kim kept eating, looking more uncomfortable by the minute.

"End of August," John said, putting his fork down and reaching across the table to squeeze Kim's hand. She looked up from her food in surprise.

Ms. Washington nearly choked on her chicken-fried steak. "That's next month!"

"I know it's fast. But I don't really see the sense in dragging out the engagement," John said. "We're in love. And besides, Tasha needs a mom."

"Maybe your mom has a point, John," Kim said, her voice low. "It takes time to plan a wedding, and Tasha—"

"Will adjust," John said, not even stopping to consider Kim's or his mother's objections. "No, I've already started looking into venues. We can definitely get married by the end of August. I won't have it any other way."

The silence then was heavy and deep. Ms. Washington looked like she wanted to reach across the table and shake her son, while Kim set down her utensils, embarrassed.

And Tasha, she was thinking of the fact that everyone in the room was talking *about* her, but not *to* her. It wasn't a great feeling.

"The last thing Tasha needs right now is any more upheaval," Ms. Washington said, her tone hard. "She had a mom, and she tragically passed before her time. She needs to heal and adjust."

"I agree," Kim said, but her voice was much lower, her words almost whisper soft.

John stabbed at his chicken-fried steak violently, upset, but said nothing, and the mood became something very, very uncomfortable.

They finished eating, and when they were done, Ms. Washington made some excuse about needing to get to bed early for an appointment in the morning. They made their way to the car, John walking them out while Kim wisely decided to hide out in the kitchen and do dishes.

Once they were outside Ms. Washington rounded on her son, her anger boiling over. "You need to slow down. You have a child now, and you need to be thinking about her."

"I am," he said, but Tasha knew John wasn't going to listen to his mom. He was used to just doing as he pleased, and no one was going to change that.

Ms. Washington opened her mouth and closed it, as though she was going to say something else, and John crossed his arms.

"All you have to do is show up to the wedding and pretend to be happy," he said, his words clipped. "I think you can manage that."

Tasha looked from her father to Ms. Washington, trying to hide her shock at the disrespectful way John spoke to his mother.

"John, I don't know what's gotten into you, but we'd best stop this conversation now before we say something we regret."

With that, Tasha and Ms. Washington got into the car and left.

As they headed back to the trailer, Ms. Washington said, "Why is that boy so anxious to get married?"

Tasha was wondering that as well. But even more confusing to her was why Kim was agreeing to it. She thought Kim could surely do better than marrying her father. And that made her wonder just why her own mom had dated John. Because now that Tasha had known him for a couple of months, he didn't seem like a very nice person.

Hopefully Kim wasn't making a terrible mistake.

Ms. Washington had just parked the car when Tasha heard the sirens.

They sounded close by and getting nearer by the moment. It was just barely light outside, the heat tolerable if still noticeable, and Ms. Washington clucked her tongue as in the distance an ambulance careened into the park. "Seems like yesterday that Old Harold passed, and now . . ."

Tasha didn't say anything, thinking of the last time the ambulance had come to the park. Had the boo hag killed again?

The ambulance turned off its siren as it drove down the dirt road, but its lights were still flashing, and heading toward them. It stopped quite a few trailers away, closer to the main office than the trailer where they lived.

"Oh no," Ms. Washington said, her face falling. "That's Greta's house. You head to the trailer and wait for me on the steps. I'm going to see what's happening."

Ms. Washington shuffled down to where a crowd was gathering in front of the gray-and-white trailer. A sick feeling settled in Tasha's middle. She wanted to go inside, to hide away, but then she saw Ellie running down the street, going to join the crowd, and she followed. She hung a bit back because she didn't want her grandmother to see that she had disobeyed her, but it didn't matter. The medics entered the trailer and then came back out quite quickly, waving everyone away and telling them to go home.

"Folks, we're going to need you to get on along. Please, for the sake of the family," said a pretty Black EMT, shouting to get everyone's attention.

A few people reluctantly stepped away, looking over their shoulders as they went, but most people stayed where they were.

"Is it the virus?" called one lady. "This is the third time in as many months."

People continued to ask questions as Tasha found Ellie on the edge of the crowd. Her eyes were wide when she turned toward Tasha, and even though it was warm, she hugged herself.

"Do you think it was the boo hag?" Ellie asked, her voice low so no one else would hear.

"I don't know," Tasha murmured. "But what else could it have been?"

The paramedics brought the body out at that moment, but it was wrapped tightly in a sheet.

Tasha's stomach tied itself in knots. "We . . . should've tried harder to find her today," she said.

Ellie nodded sadly. "Now the boo hag will have to find a new victim. We need to investigate. Do you think you could sneak out later tonight?"

Tasha blinked. "Why would we do that?"

"Because the boo hag hunts at night. This is the perfect time to discover who it might be after next," Ellie said, watching as the medics loaded Ms. Greta into the back of the ambulance.

Tasha swallowed dryly. Ellie was right. Someone had to do something, and she and Ellie were the only people who knew a boo hag was stalking the trailer park. If they didn't try to stop the creature, more people would die.

The rest of the folks who had gathered began to

leave, murmuring sadly. Their words of grief washed over Tasha like a cold shower. She couldn't help her mom; she'd been utterly powerless when she'd gotten sick. But this—this was maybe a problem she could fix.

Tasha pulled her gaze away from the body being loaded into the ambulance. "I can try."

"Meet me down by the dumpsters at ten, okay?"

Ms. Washington chose that moment to walk out of the crowd, right toward where Tasha and Ellie stood on its edges. "I thought I told you to head on back to the trailer. You don't need to see all this."

"I was just keeping Ellie company," Tasha said.

"Hi, Ms. Washington. I'm sorry about Ms. Greta. I know you were friends."

Tasha's grandmother smiled sadly and nodded at Ellie. "Thank you. I appreciate that."

"I have to get home for dinner. Later, Tash," Ellie said, waving as she left, and Ms. Washington sighed.

"I'm glad you and Ellie are friends. She's a good kid," Ms. Washington said. "Friends are important." Her expression was sad so Tasha patted the old woman's arm.

"I'm sorry about Ms. Greta too," Tasha said.

Ms. Washington's eye filled with tears. "I thought . . . I thought Greta was doing all right. I had no idea she was sick." She shook her head sadly. "Come on, I think we still have some ice cream in the freezer."

Tasha followed Ms. Washington back to the trailer, and as they walked, she tried to think of how she could sneak out of the trailer to meet Ellie. If they couldn't figure out who the boo hag was, there was no telling who the next victim would be.

16

Tasha sat on the couch in the living room as Ms. Washington watched her nighttime TV shows. It was almost ten, and she still had no idea how she was going to get out of the house to meet Ellie near the dumpsters.

Ms. Washington had never given her a bedtime, but Tasha went to bed every night at ten, just like her mom had told her to. She was thinking she could pretend to go to bed and try to sneak out of her bedroom window, but her window was just a bit too high off the ground. If she jumped out, she would almost definitely twist an ankle.

That's when she thought about where she was meeting Ellie: the dumpsters. What if she offered to take the trash out? That would be a sure way to get out of the house. And there was a good chance Ms. Washington would fall asleep in front of the TV before she got back and not even realize how long she was gone.

When her grandmother started to do the slow blink of sleepiness, Tasha stood and went to the kitchen to check the trash. It was mostly full. She pulled the bag out and tied it off. "I'm going to take out the trash," Tasha said, holding it up as she walked toward the front door.

Ms. Washington was already softly snoring. Perfect.

Tasha quietly opened and closed the front door and jogged toward the dumpsters located next to the rental office. It was creepy being out in the park in the dark, especially now that she knew that there could be a monster stalking the deep shadows in between the trailers right then. She was almost to the dumpsters when she saw Ellie running from the opposite direction. Her fear eased a little, but she still wished she was back home getting ready for bed instead of looking through the park for the boo hag.

Ellie gave her a grin as she threw away the trash. "Do you have a plan?" Tasha asked.

"Since it seems like the boo hag lives in the marsh, I was thinking we could start there. Look for clues. If it did head toward the trailer park, we might be able to track it."

"What do we do if we see it?" Tasha asked, goose bumps running along her arms at the thought.

Ellie shrugged. "I don't know. But I brought this just in case." She reached into her shorts and pulled out a tiny bottle of hot sauce. It was the tiniest bottle of hot sauce Tasha had ever seen, no bigger than her pinky.

Tasha frowned. "Hot sauce?"

"Yeah. I found some more information about boo hags on the internet. Remember how the book said that the only way to defeat a boo hag was to make sure it couldn't put its skin back on? I read that someone once put pepper in a boo hag's skin, and that kept the boo hag from putting it back on. I thought maybe hot sauce would work. I mean, this is way spicier than pepper. My aunt works on the army base and she brings these bottles home whenever she can, so we have a whole bunch of them."

Tasha nodded. "That's really smart. Good thinking."

Ellie grinned and elbowed Tasha. "I got one for you as well," she said, digging another tiny bottle of hot sauce out of her pocket.

Tasha and Ellie hurried through the park, back toward the marsh, but they'd only gone a few steps when the stench of fetid water had them skidding to a stop.

They were right in front of Ms. Washington's trailer.

Tasha grabbed Ellie's arm and dragged her back, so that they were pressed against the front of the trailer. The night was loud with the chirp of crickets and the croaking of frogs, but underneath it all was another sound, a strange clicking noise, followed by a sharp inhale.

Ellie's eyes were wide as they met Tasha's. "It's coming from the back of your trailer," she whispered, holding up her tiny bottle of hot sauce. They both quickly unwrapped the bottles, tucking the trash into their pockets. Tasha held hers up next to Ellie's, and they both nodded.

It was now or never.

Tasha's throat was thick with fear and her heart pounded as they rounded the corner of the trailer and slowly crept toward the back, their feet silent in the grass of the side yard between Ms. Washington's trailer and the one beside it. They had only taken a few steps before they froze once more, and Tasha pressed her back flat against the still-warm siding of the trailer, not far from the window to her bedroom.

There, just beyond the edge of the trailer, was a shadow that didn't quite fit. It lurched, and there the creature was, taking awkward steps as it walked along the narrow space between the trailers, lifting its knees up high as it went. The stink of fetid water and rotting fish assaulted Tasha, making her gag where she stood next to the window. A hand, the fingers too long and ending in claws, gripped the back corner of the trailer, as though the creature was going to lift itself up. Muscles bulged and flexed in the dim light between the trailers—sure enough, the creature had no skin.

The boo hag paused, like a predator sensing prey, and she and Ellie stood as still as statues. In the dim light it was possible to see the sinew and bone under the muscles, bright pale spots. The creature looked like something had stripped its skin clean away, and bile soured the back of Tasha's throat as the thing moved just right and a squelching sound came from it. The boo hag wasn't just dangerous, it was *gross*.

It evidently hadn't seen them, and Tasha held her breath to keep from making any sort of sound.

She knew they had to stop it. But its skin was nowhere in sight, and Tasha felt silly now, holding her small bottle of hot sauce while the monstrous creature with its massive claws and damp musculature

138

lurked just steps away. She couldn't move, her fear rooting her feet to the spot. She just wanted to disappear. If the boo hag saw them, they were toast.

Tasha watched in horror as the boo hag leapt up the side of the trailer, the claws making a skittering sound as the creature climbed on top of her home. It was heading toward them now—toward the louvered bathroom window someone had left open.

"Your grandma!" Ellie hissed, shocking Tasha out of her fear. They turned and ran back the way they had come, bounding up the front steps without hesitation. The boo hag couldn't get to Ms. Washington. Tasha wouldn't let it.

She burst through the front door, startling her grandmother awake where she slept in the living room chair.

"Tasha! What is going on?" Ms. Washington demanded, staggering to her feet as Ellie slammed into Tasha from behind. Tasha regained her footing and let out a breath she didn't realize she was holding.

"Um, I was taking the trash out, and I saw Ellie and . . . I was wondering if maybe she could spend the night," she said.

She expected Ms. Washington to see through her lie, but the old woman just yawned widely. "Not tonight. It's already late and it's been a busy day. Tell Ellie good night and head to bed."

Tasha turned to find Ellie staring off down the hallway to Tasha's bedroom with wide eyes. When she turned around she half expected to see the boo hag coming at them with its jerky walk—but it was John who came walking out from the back to the trailer, a frown on his face.

"Where's my duffel bag, Ma? You know, the Falcons one? I can't find it anywhere."

"John? When did you get here?" Ms. Washington asked, rubbing her eyes.

John frowned. "I told you I would be by later to get the rest of the things I left here. I mean, I still have a key. Unless you want it back?" He crossed his arms, like he wanted to continue the argument from earlier in the evening.

Ms. Washington sighed. "That bag you left is still in my closet, along with your jerseys and coat. Did you look there?"

Without answering, John turned back down the hall toward Ms. Washington's room, and Tasha turned to Ellie.

"I have to go," Ellie said, looking uncertain.

"I'll walk you out. Just in case," she said, gripping her hot sauce tighter. The fear from a few moments before was still there, but Tasha pushed through it as she followed Ellie out of the trailer.

Once on the porch, however, the night seemed completely normal. The sickening stench was gone, and there was no sign of the boo hag anywhere. A car drove down the road, heading to one of the trailers in the back.

That's when Tasha noticed John's Honda Civic was nowhere to be seen, and a strange feeling began to burble in her middle.

"Where do you think it went?" Ellie asked, looking around. "The boo hag?"

"I don't know, but we can look for clues in the morning. I have to get to bed before they start fighting," Tasha said. After so many arguments between her father and her grandmother, Tasha just wanted to avoid any more drama. "My dad and Kim are apparently getting married this summer, and my grandma isn't happy. I'm sure they're going to fight about it again."

Ellie patted her arm. "Keep the hot sauce, just in case. And be careful."

She walked back to her trailer and Tasha watched

her go for a moment before turning and heading back inside just as John was coming out, carrying a duffel bag of what must have been his clothes.

"Where's your car?" Tasha asked.

John gestured toward the front of the park. "Kim needed to borrow my car because hers is in the shop, so I walked. It's late. You need to get to bed."

John didn't bother telling her good night, just stalked off down the road, as though Tasha was somehow part of the argument he was having with his mom. She guessed she was part of it, in a way. Would John be in such a rush to marry Kim if it wasn't for having a kid to take care of?

Tasha yawned widely, feeling exhausted now that her fear had dissipated. She needed to lie down. Ms. Washington had gone back to watching her show, looking like she was about to nod off once more.

She straightened when Tasha walked past. "Make sure you brush your teeth," she said.

"Yes'm," Tasha replied.

As she walked to the bathroom, the carpet squelched under her foot, soaked through near the bathroom door. Tasha leapt back, revulsion twisting her middle as the now familiar smell of rotting fish wafted toward her.

Tasha took a step backward and stared at the puddle in the middle of the hallway.

The hallway John had just walked down moments before.

It seemed the boo hag had been in the trailer after all.

17

Tasha spent the entire night leaning against her bed-room door, the tiny hot sauce clutched in her hand. But the boo hag—could it really be John?—never returned, and eventually she fell asleep. When she woke, her body felt strange, and she realized there was a reason people had beds. Leaning against a door was no way to sleep.

In the morning Tasha headed right for Ellie's trailer once it was late enough that knocking on the door wouldn't potentially upset her aunt. But Ellie was already outside, watering her tomatoes.

"Look!" she said, holding up a single small tomato when Tasha walked up. "Do you want to try it?"

Tasha shook her head. Her muscles ached, her eyes scratchy from not getting enough sleep. "Ellie, I have to tell you something. I think . . . I think my dad might be the boo hag."

Ellie dropped her watering can, the water inside splashing all over the concrete pad in front of her trailer. "What?"

Tasha told Ellie about the wet spot in the carpet, how John hadn't been home when she left to take out the trash, and his missing car. Maybe he'd walked like he'd said—or maybe he'd ridden someone like a horse, like the book had said.

And there was more. Tasha had a lot of time to think while she was sitting up all night leaning against the bedroom door. Everything pointed to John: His frequent absences—even Kim had said he was gone all the time from her house. His presence by Ms. Greta's trailer only hours before she'd been found dead. Even the weird way he was acting about getting married, kind of like the woman they'd read about in the book. He probably wanted someone he could feed off so that he wouldn't have to hunt so much. And Kim was young; she was probably a lot tastier than the old folks in the park.

And there were other things too, Tasha realized. Like how selfish he was—definitely the sort of person who would make a deal with a witch to live forever. And the way he treated people, sucking the life out of them with worry and frustration and neglect. How long had Ms. Washington spent sitting around the trailer, wondering if he was ever going to show up? It made perfect sense.

Ellie began to pace as Tasha spoke, and when she finished, Ellie didn't say anything. She just disappeared into her house, returning with an entire box of Popsicles. "This is definitely a four-Popsicle conversation," she said, ripping one open and biting it in half.

Tasha took a Popsicle as well—cherry—but just held it in her hand. The thought of her dad hurting Kim and the other people in the park gave Tasha a stomachache, and she put the Popsicle back in the box, too nauseated to enjoy it.

"Well, there's only one thing we can do," Ellie said. "We have to find his skin, fill it with something to keep him from putting it back on, and then wait for the sun to rise so he goes—" She made a gesture like an explosion with her hands.

Tasha frowned. "I don't want to kill anyone. Especially not my dad. Ms. Washington would be devastated if something happened to him." *Even if he is a deadbeat.*

"Tasha, the boo hag killed Ms. Greta," Ellie said. "It killed who knows how many other people before her. I don't really think the boo hag is a good person. I'm sorry that it's your dad, but we can't change what he is. We have to stop him before he hurts someone else."

The thought of killing anything, even a boo hag, made Tasha feel deeply uncomfortable—the same way she'd felt when she saw the dead cat. But even so, Ellie was right. Tasha remembered the bone-numbing fear she'd felt when the creature had crawled up the side of her trailer. She never wanted to feel that way again.

And it wasn't like she'd miss John, anyway. He was never there.

"So, hot sauce or pepper in the boo hag's skin is the best way to stop them," Tasha said, thoughts spinning.

"I don't suppose you found a closet full of human skin at your grandma's house?" Ellie asked, finishing the rest of her Popsicle and grabbing another out of the box.

"No, but my grandma doesn't really want him around the house anymore. Maybe that's why he was sneaking around last night."

Ellie frowned. "What do you mean?"

"If we hadn't been looking for the boo hag, he

could've come and gone without anyone noticing, since my grandma always falls asleep in front of the TV. He could have left his skin in her room and she never would've noticed. And the bathroom window is always open, so as the boo hag he could come and go as he pleased. But now that they're fighting, he probably can't leave it at the trailer anymore because he isn't even pretending to sleep there. If my grandma caught him now, she'd be suspicious."

"So you think he moved the skin somewhere?"

Tasha nodded. "He took a duffel bag back to Kim's house. Maybe his skin was in that all along. He could've moved it for safekeeping."

Ellie nodded. "That happened with my mom when she met Ron. All her stuff ended up at his place. That's why I live with my aunt. We both lived here and she just stopped coming around. Which is fine by me, because Ron sucks." She frowned for a moment, then shook her head. "Anyway, maybe we should try to figure out how to get into Kim's house to look for the boo hag's skin. You said your dad works long hours, right?"

"Yeah, but he'd be wearing his skin then," Tasha replied. "The only time he'd take it off would be at night, when—" She didn't want to finish that sentence.

"Well, do you think we could sneak over there at night?"

Tasha stared at Ellie. "It's a long way to walk, and besides, I tell you my dad might be the boo hag and you want to sneak *into* his house?"

Ellie put her hands on her hips. "How else are we going to put hot sauce in his skin and make sure the sun catches him?"

Tasha was saved from answering by a car honking. They turned to see Kim driving down the road, John sitting in the passenger seat. Tasha did not miss the fact that Kim was driving her car, not John's.

"I guess the repair shop fixed it?" Tasha said

Ellie snorted, then whispered, "Or your dad lied."

"Hey," Kim called, waving, oblivious to the conversation between the two girls. "I was just headed to your house. We're going down to Savannah for the day. Would you like to come with us? We texted your grandmother to let her know we were going to ask you."

John didn't say anything, just slouched in his seat, his eyes obscured behind his sunglasses. Tasha thought he might be sleeping. Did he want her to come to Savannah? Or was he going along with it only because Kim wanted to invite her?

"You should go," Ellie said, her voice low. "Take the

149

chance to do some investigating. And think about my idea." She winked.

Tasha was impressed. Ellie was much braver than she was.

When she climbed into the car, Tasha was surprised to see the next book in a series she was reading in the back seat.

Kim turned around with a warm smile. "I saw that when I was at the store the other day and grabbed it. You haven't read it yet, have you?"

Tasha shook her head. "No, I haven't. Thanks!"

"Oh, good! Now buckle up."

Tasha fastened her seat belt and waved to Ellie as Kim turned the car around and they pulled away. As they drove out of the park, Tasha eyed the back of John's seat warily. She really, really wished her father wasn't a boo hag. Because she could get used to having Kim as a stepmom. She missed her mom terribly, but having Kim around made Tasha feel less lonely.

She would have to find a way to be brave like Ellie. Otherwise, Kim might suffer the same fate as Ms. Greta.

The drive to Savannah was short. Tasha only had the chance to read two chapters in her book before they were pulling into a parking garage. As they did, Kim chattered about Savannah's history while Tasha's father, slouching in the passenger seat, nodded along and yawned widely.

Tasha had just seen her father the night before, and he hadn't looked anything like this. He was exhausted. There were noticeable bags under his eyes, and his skin had an almost grayish cast. Was it because he hadn't found a new victim since Ms. Greta died? Did boo hags start to get worn down when they hadn't been able to feed? Tasha didn't know, she didn't remember the book discussing it, but it would explain why he looked so tired.

Kim didn't seem to notice, and John did perk up a bit as they started to walk around. Kim led them from picturesque square to picturesque square, reading historical markers aloud and pointing at all the quaint little houses tucked here and there. Tasha found it hard not to share Kim's enthusiasm. Savannah was a pretty cool place, and Tasha actually liked history.

"Oh!" Kim exclaimed as they exited a square onto a small lane lined with little shops and restaurants. "I want to go in and look at that dress. I'll be right back."

John nodded with a jaw-cracking yawn, leaned up against the building, and closed his eyes. Tasha was going to follow Kim into the store when a sign in the window of one nearby caught her eye: "The World's Strongest Hot Sauce."

She went over to examine the shop. A stronger hot sauce would definitely be handy. It was almost as if she was meant to come on this trip. For some reason, at that moment she thought of her mom. Not because she liked hot sauce—though she did—but because it felt like a sign. If her mom was up in heaven watching like everyone kept telling Tasha she was, surely she knew about the boo hag. The hot sauce shop seemed like her mom reaching out to help her.

"Hey, where are you going?" John asked, suddenly at her side.

"I want to check out this hot sauce shop," Tasha said.

John's eyebrows rose. "I didn't know you like hot sauce."

"I just wanted to see if I recognized any of the labels. Mom liked super-extra-spicy hot sauce, and we would take turns trying out the spiciest ones she could find." It wasn't the real reason Tasha wanted to check out the hot sauce shop, but it was the truth.

John's face fell just a bit and he nodded. "Yeah. She did always like really spicy things. When she was pregnant with you, we'd go eat these hot wings that were just . . . .whew! She would finish her whole plate, but I never could."

His gaze went far away then, and without thinking about it, Tasha's head filled with so many questions she'd wanted to ask him. If he'd ever loved her mother. If he had, why he'd abandoned them.

There was so much she didn't know about John, and in that moment, Tasha wanted desperately for him to say something, anything, that would prove he wasn't a monster.

But the moment passed, and John seemed to shake

153

himself. "Anyway, that was a while ago, and we don't have time to mess about in a hot sauce shop. Come on, let's go eat lunch."

Annoyance welled up in Tasha. She hated that she had to explain everything to John, and even when she did, he didn't listen. Everything had to be exactly what he wanted, always. It was just like when they'd first met, in those dark days after her mom's death, and he'd always been confused by whatever she did, as though he'd never met a kid before.

The memory made a sudden lump rise in her throat. John's expression softened and he shrugged. "Fine. If you want to go and look at the hot sauce, go ahead. But I'm not buying you anything. I hate spicy foods. Can't eat 'em anymore."

Tasha narrowed her eyes. *Of course you don't like spicy foods*, she thought. *You're a boo hag.* It made her even more determined to get a bottle of hot sauce from the store. She didn't have any money, but maybe she could benefit from a little divine intervention.

Tasha turned on her heel and walked into the hot sauce shop, John following reluctantly.

The old Black man behind the counter looked up from his newspaper as Tasha walked in, his dark face breaking into a wide smile amid his snowy beard. "Hello there, young lady. Can I help you?"

"Just looking," she said.

The bells on the door rang again as Kim entered right behind them, a frown on her face. "I saw you head this way. Were you really going to buy hot sauce without me?"

Tasha shook her head. "I was just looking."

"I already told her I wasn't going to buy her anything. She said she just wanted to look," John said, crossing his arms. "Something about her and her mom having hot sauce challenges."

Kim touched his arm gently. "Nonsense. Tasha, if you want to pick out some hot sauce, I'll get it for you."

Tasha had to keep herself from smiling in triumph. "What's the hottest sauce you have?" she asked the store clerk.

He reached into the case and pulled out a bottle with a plain black label with a skull and crossbones on it. "Reaper XL. One drop will burn the taste buds right out of your mouth—and yet leave you hankering for more!"

Kim looked at Tasha. "Sound good?"

At Tasha's nod, John sighed. "I already told her no. She doesn't need super-hot sauce."

Kim gave John a gentle smile. "It's a small thing, John. It'll make her happy."

Tasha shifted her weight from foot to foot, feeling embarrassed and uncomfortable, but also relieved that Kim was on her side. At least she got it.

John was pouting like a little kid, but Kim didn't even seem to notice. Was she under some kind of spell? Had John already begun stealing her soul, making her mind foggy?

Kim turned back to the man behind the counter. "How much?" she asked.

"If you pay cash, I'll give it to you for twenty."

Kim pulled a twenty-dollar bill from her purse and handed it to the man. He gave the bottle to Tasha.

"There," Kim said, as though that put an end to the argument. "Do you want to go get some lunch? I'm starving."

Tasha nodded and didn't even bother to glance at her father as they left the shop.

"What are you going to eat your hot sauce on?" Kim asked, and Tasha shrugged.

"I don't know. I think I'm going to save it for a special occasion," she said.

Kim nodded. "Well, I hope I'm around when you open it. I suspect it got its name from the Carolina

Reaper, one of the hottest peppers in the world. It should be something!"

John said nothing, just followed them sullenly. Tasha's stomach churned as they made their way to a pizza place for lunch, and she avoided looking at her father for the rest of the day. Tasha made certain to stay close to Kim, her hot sauce tucked under her arm.

In the brief time she'd known her, Kim had taken care of Tasha—now it was up to Tasha to keep her safe.

19

The day after the awkward trip to Savannah, Tasha woke groggy and annoyed. She'd tried sleeping in her bed, but every little creak of the trailer or wheeze of the air-conditioner had her sitting straight up, heart pounding, the bottle of Reaper XL clutched in her hands. She finally nodded off, back against the bedroom door once more.

Ms. Washington found her there in the morning, opening the door into her spine as she asked if Tasha wanted sausage or scrambled eggs. As Tasha groaned, the older woman clucked her tongue.

"Tasha. What are you doing up against the door like that?"

"I couldn't sleep, and I thought it might be more comfortable to sit up," Tasha said drowsily. Ms.

158

Washington just shook her head with a smile and went to make breakfast.

And then there was a knock at the door, too early to be a stranger. The door opened a bit and Kim stuck her head inside.

"Knock-knock!" she called. "Good morning, y'all."

"Kim. You're right on time," Ms. Washington said, putting the patties on a paper towel. "Sausage?"

"Oh, none for me," Kim said, getting a mug and pouring herself a cup of coffee. Tasha kept waiting for Ms. Washington to snap at her, but she just seemed resigned to Kim being in her space, making herself comfortable. Tasha felt like she'd missed something.

"What's up?" Tasha asked. "Is everything okay with my dad?"

"We're supposed to go dress shopping today," Kim said. "Did you forget?"

"No, I did," Ms. Washington said. "I've been so tired that it completely slipped my mind!"

A worried look darkened Kim's expression, her pale brow wrinkling. "I'm sorry, Tasha. I was going to go wedding dress shopping today, and I was wondering if you might like to come along. But if you have other plans—"

"No, it sounds like fun," Tasha said. She could use a break from all the stuff with the boo hag. Shopping for wedding dresses with Kim would be better than worrying how she was going to get her hands on John's boo hag skin.

"Tasha, how about some pancakes?" Ms. Washington asked. "You're going to have a long morning ahead of you."

"Sure," Tasha said, taking a seat at the kitchen table while her grandma pulled a box of pancake mix from the cupboard.

"What's wrong? You seem kind of down," Kim said, taking the chair opposite at the kitchen table.

"Nothing," Tasha said.

Ms. Washington clucked her tongue again. "Someone didn't sleep last night," she said.

"It was just a nightmare," Tasha muttered, feeling silly.

"Oh, I'm sorry. Stress can sometimes do that, and I'm sure all this wedding talk has got you as nervous as it has me. Is there something I can do to help?"

Tasha just shook her head. She wanted to tell Kim to get as far away from John as she could, that the marriage was a terrible idea, and not for the reasons Ms. Washington thought. She couldn't say anything,

160

though, because how would she explain herself? She just got up and went to the fridge, grabbing the orange juice and pouring herself a glass. She could feel both Ms. Washington and Kim watching her, and for some reason that made her even more uncomfortable.

"I was thinking . . . you could spend the night at my house," Kim said just as Ms. Washington began to pour batter into the pan. "Maybe the change would feel a little less scary if you had a chance to get to know the place a bit. And a change of scenery couldn't hurt if you're having trouble sleeping."

Tasha tried to keep the excitement off her face as she drank her orange juice. This was exactly what Ellie had suggested, a chance to try and find John's skin in the place he'd most likely keep it when he would leave to hunt. And here Kim was, handing Tasha the opportunity without her even having to ask. It was like more divine intervention.

Maybe Tasha's mom was looking out for her after all.

Ms. Washington nodded. "It's a good idea. A change of scenery, like Kim said." Ms. Washington yawned and sighed. "And since you'll be over at Kim's, I can go to bed a bit earlier. I haven't been sleeping well, and I should try to catch up on sleep."

Tasha stared at her grandmother, remembering how Ms. Greta had complained about having trouble sleeping. Her grandma flipped the pancakes one last time before putting them on a plate with a sausage patty and setting both in front of Tasha.

And when she did, Tasha spotted the marks on her arm. Just like the ones on Ms. Greta's.

Tasha couldn't stop the tremble that started up in her hands as her grandmother moved languidly about the kitchen. She chewed slowly, carefully, while Kim chattered to Ms. Washington about dresses.

How could he? How could John steal his own mother's life? Tasha knew her dad was selfish and irresponsible, but this? This was too much.

Still, she knew she wasn't wrong. He was never nice to his mom. After all, he had dumped Tasha on her. And she remembered the way John had talked to Ms. Washington after he announced his engagement to Kim. He should appreciate having a mom as long as she was around.

How long had he been preying on her? Had it just started? Or had John slowly been draining the life from his mom for years?

Tasha gripped her fork so hard that she felt the metal bend a bit. She had to stop him. She had to find a way to be brave, to find where he hid his skin while he was hunting and douse it with the entire bottle of Reaper XL.

Kim apparently also noticed that Ms. Washington didn't look well. "Mary, do you want me to clean up the kitchen so you can rest? You look like you could use a break after cooking such a delicious breakfast."

Ms. Washington swayed a bit on her feet. "You know, I will take you up on that offer. Thank you." She shuffled to the living room.

"Kim, do you mind if my friend Ellie comes to stay the night at your house too?" Tasha said. "We'd been planning to have a sleepover here, but Ms. Washington has been too tired."

Kim smiled brightly as she loaded the dishwasher. "That's a fantastic idea! John has plans tonight, so we can make it a girls' night. We'll get pizza and watch whatever you want. I even have some really pretty nail polish colors that I've been saving for a special occasion, if you'd like to paint our nails. And if you bring your hot sauce, we can try it out." Kim gave her a conspiratorial smile. "Your dad won't be around for dinner, so we can make it as spicy as we want."

Tasha forced a smile in return. "That sounds great," she said, even as fear surged through her. John must be planning to hunt, and if so, it would give them just the opportunity they needed to find his skin. But it also meant that Ms. Washington would be in danger.

Whatever they were going to do, it had to happen tonight.

After a morning of putting on and taking off dresses, Kim took Tasha to lunch at a fried chicken place. She wasn't sure what to order, so Kim got spicy strips for both of them.

"A little practice for tonight, right?" she said.

Tasha nodded, and a warm feeling suffused her, until she thought again about what they were doing tonight. As afraid as she was, she was also eager for night to come. She wanted to know where John left his skin when he went out to hunt, how hard it would be to find it, how they would distract Kim so that they could douse it with hot sauce.

Tasha took a deep breath and sighed. She would deal with the whole mess later. She still had to see if Ellie could get permission to come to the sleepover.

There was no way Tasha could take on the boo hag by herself.

The chicken strips were good, but a little too spicy. Tasha knew right then she wasn't going to actually eat the hot sauce at the sleepover with Kim. She would die.

As they ate, an awkward silence fell over the table. Kim finally pushed her empty box to the side. "Sweetheart, is something wrong? You seem a bit off today."

Tasha shifted in her seat.

"You know you can tell me anything, right?" she said.

"Anything?" Tasha asked.

Kim nodded and smiled. "Of course. What's going on?"

Tasha had to warn Kim. She was in danger, just like Ms. Washington. Maybe Kim didn't have any marks on her arms yet, but it was only a matter of time, and if Tasha couldn't find John's boo hag skin and stop him, well . . . she at least had to tell Kim that she was in danger, somehow.

Tasha's stomach gurgled, whether from what she was about to say or the spicy chicken strips, she wasn't quite sure. "I . . . don't think you should marry my dad," Tasha said. It wasn't what she wanted to say, but it was the best she could do.

Kim's face fell, and she leaned back. "Oh. Okay. Can you tell me why?"

"It's just that . . . John isn't a good person," Tasha said. She couldn't exactly tell Kim that he was a *monster*. Would she even believe in something like a boo hag without seeing it? Tasha hadn't.

"So you're saying you don't think he's good enough for . . . me?"

"Yes! He doesn't help my grandma around the house—he just leaves his shoes in the middle of the floor and can't even be bothered to fold up his blanket in the morning. And that's when he even bothers to stop by. Plus, you know, he walked out on my mom when I was just a baby. I'm pretty sure he's a *deadbeat*."

Kim didn't respond, so Tasha continued on.

"Anyway, I don't think you should marry him. You're really nice, and you should find someone who is also really nice."

At that, Kim sniffled and nodded. Tasha felt bad. She hadn't wanted to upset her, but what would happen to Kim if she married John? He'd only drain the life out of her, slowly.

After a moment, Kim reached across the table to take Tasha's hand. "Well, that is something, and I thank you. You're a great kid, Tasha. You should know that. Do you want to know what I think?"

Tasha nodded.

"I think that you and your dad still need to get to know one another. The truth is, your dad isn't perfect, but really, no one is, especially not me. I know you don't believe this, but under the surface, your dad has a lot of really good traits. I love John, I know he's going to be a great husband, and I believe he can learn to be a better dad if we just give him a chance. People can change, and we have to give them that chance to do better."

Tasha wanted to argue. She wanted to tell Kim that her father had always been the person he was, that he was never going to change, especially not now. But something about Kim's sad, hopeful smile made her realize it would be futile. She wasn't going to listen to a kid about this sort of thing.

It was up to Tasha to stop her father before it was too late.

Kim began to gather the trash. "I'm really glad you came dress shopping with me. I'll drop you back off at home—you can talk to Ellie about staying the night, and if it's all right, I'll pick you both up around six, okay?"

The ride back to the trailer park was quiet, just the radio filling the silence, and Tasha found herself hoping that Kim wasn't mad at her for saying what she said. How would she feel if someone told her not to marry the person she loved? Probably not great.

But when Kim dropped her off in front of Ms. Washington's trailer, she looked like her usual happy self again. "If Ellie's aunt has any questions, please tell her she can call me. Ms. Washington has my number. I'm going to pick up some snacks now—this sleepover is going to be epic."

Kim drove off and Tasha waited until her car was out of sight before making her way down to Ellie's trailer.

Ellie was sweeping her patio. "There you are! I went to find you earlier and your grandma said you went dress shopping."

"Yeah, but there's more. Kim invited me to spend the night—and said I could bring you. Plus, she said my dad already told her he's going to be out tonight. This is our chance to find the boo hag's skin and stop it, once and for all. Just like you said yesterday."

Ellie jumped up and down. "Perfect! My aunt's asleep right now, but when she wakes up I'll ask if I can spend the night. We're going to need a plan. I'm thinking one of us should distract your dad's fiancée while the other one looks for the boo hag skin."

Tasha nodded. "I also got some extra-spicy hot sauce we can use. If anything can keep a boo hag out of its skin, it'll be this stuff."

"Great. I have to finish up my chores but I'll come by once I know if I can go."

Tasha nodded and ran back to her trailer, her anxiousness lending her speed. She needed to check on her grandma.

Ms. Washington was snoring in the living room easy chair when Tasha got back. Tasha didn't want to bother her so she moved through the trailer as quietly as possible. Her first task was to pack an overnight bag. She made sure to grab the Reaper XL, plus the tiny bottle Ellie had given her. She also decided to snag another backup, one of the many bottles of hot sauce her grandmother kept in the cupboard. There was no telling what might happen.

When she went to the kitchen, she discovered that Ms. Washington was no longer in her easy chair. Tasha eventually found her in her bed, snoring heavily. Tasha pulled the covers up so that Ms. Washington was all tucked in, then grabbed her bag and went to the living room to wait.

Tasha tried watching TV, tried reading, but couldn't focus on anything. Soon, there was a knock at the door.

Ellie stood there, grinning, her overnight bag hanging off her shoulder. "Let's sauce this hag," she said.

Tasha's nervousness lessened, just a bit. At least she wouldn't have to face the monster alone.

21

Kim arrived a short while after Ellie did, and they left for her house in high spirits. Kim was just as kind and welcoming to Ellie as she had been to Tasha, and once everyone had been introduced, the girls piled into the back seat while Kim drove the short way to her place, outside of the trailer park and just a little ways down the road.

"We probably could've walked," Kim said with a laugh. "If it wasn't so hot, that is."

A few minutes later they were pulling down the long driveway. Tasha and Ellie climbed out, hefting their overnight bags, while Kim opened the door for them and closed it once they were inside.

On the kitchen counter was an array of snacks, including potato chips and chocolate, but most impressive was the jelly beans. Kim gestured to the bounty. "I got some snacks, but I wasn't sure what kind of candy you liked best, so I got a little bit of everything," she said.

"Jelly beans are my favorite," Tasha said.

Kim beamed. "Mine too!" she said. "This is going to be such a fun night."

After they finished eyeing the snack stash, Kim led them down the hall. "Tasha, this is going to be your room, once you move in. It still needs some decorations, but the bed is big enough to share for tonight. Unless you girls want to sleep in the living room?"

Ellie responded by dropping her bag in the corner and flopping dramatically onto the bed. "This bed is great," she said.

"I think we're sleeping in here tonight," Tasha said.

"Great. Well, you girls wash your hands—I'm thinking we can make cookies," Kim said. "Meet me in the kitchen."

Ellie and Tasha made their way to the bathroom across the hall. As they washed up, Ellie kept glancing at Tasha in the mirror.

"What?" Tasha asked.

"Your dad's already gone," Ellie murmured.

"Yeah, he's probably at work or out with his friends right now," Tasha said, her voice also low.

Ellie nodded. "I was thinking maybe we should try looking in the closets."

"He wouldn't be hunting yet."

"I know, but still, we might be able to find where he keeps his skin when he's out."

They finished washing up and found Kim in the kitchen, scooping chocolate chip dough out of a package and onto a cookie sheet. It wasn't homemade like Ms. Washington's cookie dough, but Tasha wasn't going to complain. Cookies were cookies.

There was the sound of keys in the door, and Tasha's father walked in.

Ellie stiffened next to Tasha and grabbed her arm. "He looks awful," she whispered as Kim put the cookies in the oven and walked into the living room to greet John.

Ellie was right. He looked gray and washed out, but he summoned a smile for Tasha. "Hey, kiddo. Glad you made it. Who's your friend?"

"This is Ellie," Kim said. Neither Ellie nor Tasha moved from their spot at the kitchen counter, and Tasha could feel a nervous tremble in Ellie's hand.

"Ellie. Nice to meet you," John said with a yawn. "I just stopped by because I need my phone charger.

Give me a moment and I'll leave you girls to your fun."

John headed off to the bedroom and returned moments later, kissing Kim on the cheek before leaving. Tasha felt a prickle of rage. Once again, John was walking away while she was right here.

It almost made her more mad than the fact that he was a boo hag. Almost.

Tasha didn't have long to worry about her father. It turned out that Kim had a whole evening planned. Pizza, a movie, and board games. The pizza was pepperoni, her favorite; the movie was *Toy Story*, also her favorite; and the game was Sorry—not her favorite, but Ellie loved it, and it turned out to be a lot of fun.

"Here comes the green machine!" Ellie said every time she either got to slide into someone else's piece or bump them back home. It could have gotten annoying to Tasha if it were anyone else doing it, but she found it funny when it was Ellie, especially when she got to do it back. Tasha was even able to stop worrying about her dad and her grandma for a bit.

It didn't last.

With Kim having every moment planned, and

keeping a watchful eye on them, there hadn't been time for either of them to sneak off. And the later it got, the more Tasha despaired about being able to actually stop her father.

Finally, after their fifth game of Sorry, Ellie yawned widely. "I think I need to go to sleep."

Tasha nodded. The clock in the kitchen read after midnight. She hadn't stayed up that late since before her mom got sick. She was actually tired—but she was also pretty sure that Ellie was putting on an act for Kim's benefit. They still had to find the boo hag's skin.

Maybe they could sneak into Kim and John's bedroom once Kim was asleep. It was a long shot, but Tasha was hopeful that between the two of them they could work out a plan.

Kim nodded and started putting away the game pieces. "Well then, I suppose you should go and brush your teeth. Let me know if you need anything, okay?"

Ellie and Tasha slowly made their way to the bedroom.

"Okay, where's the hot sauce?" Ellie said, her voice entirely too loud. Tasha shushed her before getting the bottle out and handing it to her.

"How are we supposed to sneak into their bedroom?" Tasha asked. "Kim didn't seem tired yet at all."

"We can set an alarm on my phone, and wake up in three hours," Ellie said, holding up her phone. "That'll be three a.m. She won't stay up that long, will she?"

Tasha shrugged. "I don't know. I've never spent the night here before."

Ellie pursed her lips. "Okay, well, it's the best plan we've got. Let's turn out the lights—if she thinks we're asleep, she's more likely to go to bed. Then, while she's sleeping, we can sneak into the room."

They put their pajamas on and climbed into the big bed. Tasha had never been in such a comfy bed, and she could feel her bones turn to jelly as soon as she lay down. She was so tired. She hadn't slept much the two nights before, not since they'd seen the boo hag scale the side of Ms. Washington's trailer, and she found it impossible to keep her eyes open.

"Too bad about your dad," Ellie murmured as they dozed off. "Kim would be a cool mom."

Tasha didn't say anything, sleep too heavy to resist as her eyelids lowered, but she was afraid that Ellie was right. Maybe, just maybe, Kim would still want to hang out with her after her dad was gone.

22

Tasha jerked suddenly out of sleep. She didn't remember having a nightmare, and yet she woke with the same heart-pounding sensation as she did when she'd dreamt something terrible.

The first thing she noticed was the smell. A wet, gross stench like dead fish and spoiled milk. It smelled so familiar, and that was when Tasha realized it was the same marsh stink that always accompanied the boo hag. Fear stiffened her limbs.

"Tasha."

Tasha blinked and started to sit up, but Ellie's hand on her arm kept her in place.

"Don't move."

Ellie was whispering, but her voice was trembling in terror.

Tasha's eyes began to adjust to the darkness, and she could finally see what Ellie did.

Someone was standing at the foot of the bed.

No. Not someone. Some *thing*.

The light from the moon out the window was weak, but there was no mistaking the silhouette. It looked like it had before—long hair and a vaguely human shape—but this time sickly green eyes glowed where the face should have been. Tasha could *feel* that the thing was dangerous, like being startled by a snake hiding in the grass.

She waited, breathing heavily, right along with Ellie. The thing hadn't moved. It was just standing there, staring at them.

It shifted slightly toward them and a clicking sound came from the creature's throat. When the boo hag began to bend over them, Tasha couldn't hold herself still any longer.

She kicked upward swiftly, the covers coming off her and Ellie and lifting up and onto the creature. The boo hag shrieked and fell back toward the wall, scrabbling at the blanket. It threw it off, and then sunk its clawed hands and feet into the wall. The creature climbed up and onto the ceiling like some giant spider, looking down on the girls with its horrible, sunken glowing eyes.

"Go, go!" Tasha yelled.

The girls tumbled off the bed, sprinting out of the room in terror.

"We need the hot sauce," Ellie said as Tasha led the way to the back bedroom. "Then find the skin and get out of the house. We can worry about destroying it once we're safe."

"We have to find Kim first!" Tasha said. "We can't leave without her."

The door to John and Kim's bedroom was ajar, light coming through the small crack. The girls piled into the room, and Tasha slammed the door shut and twisted the lock behind them.

Her heart was pounding painfully, and her thoughts raced. "Why did it just stand there?" Tasha asked. "How long was it there before I woke up?"

"I don't know. I woke up only a minute before you did," Ellie said. She was strangely calm, and she pointed to something over Tasha's shoulder. "Look. The closet. This is our chance."

"We have to find Kim," Tasha said, and Ellie gestured to the room.

"She's not here, so maybe she went out or something. We can search for the skins and then go find her."

Tasha nodded and turned on the light and then went over to the room's only closet while Ellie leaned against the door, bracing it. It would be weird to search through Kim's private things while examining her dad's possessions, but she didn't really have a choice.

The closet door slid open easily, and Tasha was confronted with dozens of hanging dresses, a few of which she recognized from seeing Kim wear them. A moment later, a smell hit her, one that made Tasha pause.

"Tash," Ellie called. "I can't hear the boo hag anymore." Tasha didn't have a chance to respond before Ellie was standing next to her, pinching her nose. "Ugh, what is that smell?"

Tasha shook her head. "I don't know. Nothing good." She took a not-so-deep breath and pushed the dresses to the side so she could see the very back of the closet. There, hanging limply, were several bodysuits made of some strange material. They were pinned to hangers and looked a little bit like pantyhose: thin, pliable, the color of flesh—

Tasha felt something awful in her belly.

"Oh my god," Ellie said, breathless. "Are those . . . ?"

"Skins," Tasha said, willing herself not to puke.

There was too much saliva in her mouth and her hands began to shake. "There are . . . so many of them."

Tasha had seen a snake shed its skin once. These looked something like that, and yet nothing like that at all. Beside them was the gray pelt of some animal. Tasha's stomach fell and she felt nauseated. "What color did you say that cat was?"

"Gray . . ." Ellie trailed off and they looked at one another in horror.

Next to the gray pelt was a fluffy black-and-white scrap of fur and Tasha gestured to it. "I guess we know what happened to poor Fredo," she said, voice low.

"What do we do?" Ellie asked, taking a step backward. "Let's just find Kim and get out of here!"

Tasha shook her head and pointed at the skin that hung in front of all the others—the freshest-looking one. The color of the skin was light, and it had long brown hair hanging from the top.

"I think . . . he got her," she whispered.

Ellie's eyes went wide and filled with tears. "We have to go," she whispered, fear riding every syllable. "Or we're going to be next."

In that moment, hearing the terror in Ellie's voice, Tasha realized she wasn't afraid. She was *angry*. Without thinking, she grabbed a canvas tote bag off a hook in the back of the closet and reached for the skins. They felt cool and alive when she touched them, a bit like picking up a worm in the grass, and they wriggled in her arms as she shoved them into the bag.

Ellie gaped. "What are you doing?"

"One of these is John's skin. The rest he must use for repairs, or . . . I don't know, trophies or something. Destroying one of them won't be enough. We need to put hot sauce in all of them."

"Our hot sauce is in the bedroom," Ellie said. "What if the boo hag is still in there, waiting for us? I don't think we should try going back that way."

"We can head to my house. It's not that far back to the trailer park. We can get the hot sauce from my grandma's trailer and use that." She didn't mention that was where the boo hag might be heading as well.

Ellie snapped her fingers. "Good thinking. Let's get out of here."

Tasha snapped the bag shut as the skins began to struggle in earnest. The things were more alive than she'd thought, and she tried to ignore the way they thrashed in the bag as she hoisted it onto her shoulder.

Then she took the lead, opening the door slowly to check the hallway. Most of the lights were off, casting the house in shadow. But the kitchen light burned brightly, and the front of the house appeared to be empty. Safe.

They ran toward the entrance, Tasha stopping momentarily in the kitchen to grab the jelly beans off the counter. At Ellie's skeptical look, she shrugged.

"Something I read in *A Guide to Southern Myths and Legends* about swamp witches. I hope jelly beans count."

Tasha took off in a run, Ellie not far behind. They ran up the driveway, the bag with the skins bouncing painfully against Tasha's hip. She slapped it once and the skins seemed to calm down.

The distance back to the park was not far, but they were exhausted, and their footsteps were uncertain on the dark road. They ran until Ellie got a stitch, and then they hobbled along as quickly as they could, every little sound from within the trees that lined the road and pressed in all around making them jump in terror.

They were almost to the main road that led through the trailer park when they heard a commotion in the nearby woods—a crashing, thrashing sound that could only be made by something big. Ellie grabbed Tasha's arm and pulled her off the road toward a wide oak tree.

They both ducked down, and that was when John came stumbling out of the woods. His expression was dazed, but otherwise, he looked normal.

The world seemed to tilt, and Ellie gripped Tasha's arm. "How did he get his skin back? Was it not one of the ones in the closet after all?"

Tasha's heart pounded, lodging in her chest just as a sickly, decaying-fish smell hit them.

With the crash of breaking branches, the boo hag erupted out of the trees. It landed on John's back, and he gave a horrible grunt. A moment later, his body bent in a strange way, his spine popping and throbbing as his shirt ripped. He leaned over on all fours like a dog, his arms lengthening and spine reforming until he looked like a person who had been stretched and reshaped into a horse.

The boo hag was riding Tasha's father.

"But if your dad isn't the boo hag," Ellie whispered, "then the skins in the closet—"

"They weren't his," Tasha finished. They could only have belonged to the other person that lived in the house.

Kim's skin, the one they'd found hanging in the closet—it hadn't been there because John had killed her and skinned her.

It was there because the boo hag had taken it off. To hunt.

The hag screeched and John took off, galloping

down the main road toward the trailer park. The girls stayed hidden for a few more heartbeats after the boo hag was out of sight, and Tasha stood, her stomach burbling.

"We have to go back," she said.

Ellie frowned. "Back where? To that thing's house?"

Tasha nodded. "She must be heading to my grandma's trailer. There's no guarantee we'll be able to get her hot sauce. We need the stuff we brought."

They ran back the way they'd come, moving faster this time, fear quickening their pace. Tasha tried not to feel the bitter edge of disappointment that swallowed her, the only emotion that could keep up with her fear. *Kim is the boo hag.* Tasha's heart was breaking, and she wanted to sit down on the ground and cry. She thought she'd finally found someone who understood her, who was willing to try, and it was a monster who fed on people.

She had been wrong. Her father might be a jerk, but he wasn't the boo hag.

Their steps slowed as they approached the house. What had seemed lovely and unassuming in the daylight felt ominous in the wee hours of the morning, now that they knew it was the den of a boo hag. The shadows seemed deeper, the hoots of a far-off owl spookier.

They retraced their steps through the kitchen, the skins kicking up a fit as they went. Tasha struggled to hold them in place while Ellie pushed past her, going to the bedroom that would have been Tasha's if John and Kim had gotten married. If Kim wasn't a monster.

If, if, if. Tasha pushed the strange yearning she felt to the side. She had to save her grandmother. And, she realized, John as well. And the only way to do that was to stop Kim once and for all. Even if she did really, really like her.

When they got to Tasha's room, it was to find that the room had been demolished. The bed was upended, the walls had been slashed, and their bags had been torn to shreds—there was no hot sauce to be found.

Ellie and Tasha stood in the doorway, frozen at the carnage before them. "I guess it's a good thing we ran," Ellie whispered.

Tasha shook her head, took a deep breath, and let it out. "Okay, hot sauce is a no. But the key to beating the hag is to make sure she doesn't have her skin on when the sun rises, right? Maybe there's something else we can use on these things."

Ellie nodded. "Yeah, okay, okay. If we can't make them so that she can't put them on . . . can't we just destroy them? Like, burn them?"

Tasha nodded. "We could put them on the barbe-cue grill?"

"Good thinking," Ellie said. "Let's go."

They ran back the way they had come, heading outside. Tasha and Ellie made their way around to the side yard where the grill was. The light from the kitchen window cast a glow onto the patio.

The grill was an old one with a propane tank, and they both stared at it, perplexed.

"Do you know how to turn it on?" Ellie asked.

Tasha shook her head. "My mom never let me near the grill. She said it was dangerous."

"Yeah, well, in this case I think the skinless monster who turned your dad into a weird horse is the bigger threat," Ellie said as she started twisting the knobs.

"I'm guessing the red button lights it," Tasha said.

Ellie pushed the red button and there was a click-ing sound followed by a slight *whoosh*.

"The flames don't look very high," Tasha said, lean-ing in to look at the grill. "Do you think it'll—"

But she couldn't finish the thought before there was a clicking noise from behind them.

The girls spun around. There, hulking at the edge of the patio, was the boo hag.

The light from the house washed over the hideous

thing, illuminating details that Tasha hadn't been able to see before in the dark. Its sunken, glowing green eyes were too large for its face, which looked uncannily smooth. The arms were too long, and the fingers were easily twice as long as a normal woman's. Each finger ended in a razor-sharp glistening black claw, and Tasha wondered if that was how the boo hag skinned her victims. It was definitely how she'd destroyed Tasha's room. But worst of all was the oozing red musculature that made up the boo hag's body. Thick blood dropped off the creature where it stood, splattering on the concrete wetly, and the bones and tendons shone white in the light. What Tasha had thought was hair actually looked to be veins, set adrift without skin to keep them in place. A few pulsed, and Tasha felt fresh nausea roil her belly.

She couldn't believe this thing had been inside Kim's skin the entire time.

Tasha pulled the skins from the tote bag and threw them on the grill, slamming the lid closed and turning the knobs all the way up. A strange scream came from the grill.

At that, the boo hag shrieked as well. The sound was terrifying, and Tasha and Ellie slammed their hands over their ears.

"Tasha! Please." The voice, now, was Kim's, but

distorted, like her throat was filled with broken glass, each word harsh and sharp. "It doesn't have to be like this. Give them back to me."

"No!" Tasha yelled, Ellie helping to hold the lid down on the grill as the skins writhed and howled. What had Kim done to the people she'd skinned? Were their souls somehow caught inside their remains? The more Tasha learned about the boo hag, the more horrified she felt. "You killed all those people. I won't let you hurt my grandma. Or my dad."

In that moment, Tasha remembered the bag of jelly beans tucked under her arm. She let go of the grill lid and ripped the package open, the beans going in every direction. The world seemed to freeze as the boo hag's eyes widened, watching as the beans fell to the ground.

The huge creature fell to her knees and began frantically gathering them.

"I . . . What did you do?" Ellie asked.

"I read it in my grandmother's book. If you scatter beans in front of a witch, they have to pick up each bean and count them all. When I saw the jelly beans, I thought it was worth a try."

While the boo hag was distracted, Tasha and Ellie found a couple of bungee cords in the nearby shed and secured the lid to the grill. Already the skins had quieted down but thick smoke emanated from the edges of the lid, the acrid plume making the girls cough. The boo hag looked up at the grill in fear, but she couldn't stop what she was doing. Tears streamed down her face, and Tasha watched in terror and sadness as she counted, powerless to stop the inevitable.

Once it was clear that the skins had burned away, they stayed only long enough to watch as the first rays of sunlight peeked through the trees that surrounded the cottage. There were still quite a few jelly beans scattered about, and Ellie pointed up at the sky.

"I don't think she's going to finish in time," she said, her voice low. "And her skins are charcoal."

Ellie was right. And whatever the sun would do to Kim, even if she was the boo hag, was not something Tasha wanted to see.

"I'm sorry," Tasha whispered as Ellie pulled her toward the road. The girls ran all the way to the trailer park and Tasha never looked back once.

The sunrise would take care of what was left of the boo hag. Everyone was safe.

23

By the time the girls got back to the trailer park, the
sun was completely up. The run had felt longer than it
was, and Tasha kept expecting the boo hag to appear
out of nowhere. But everything was calm.

"Do you want to go back to my house so you don't
get in trouble?" Tasha asked.

Ellie nodded. "Yeah, that's probably best. I don't
know what I'm going to tell my aunt about my overnight bag, though. Maybe I'll just say I lost it."

Tasha smiled. "You could just blame it on a murder ghost."

Ellie laughed. "Nah, those aren't real."

They trudged down the trailer park's main road,
sneaking past Ellie's trailer even though it was too
early for anyone to be up. By the time they got closer
to Ms. Washington's trailer, Tasha was bone tired, and

as she climbed the front steps, she didn't even register that the lights were all on and the front door was ajar.

"Is that . . . normal?" Ellie asked.

Tasha shook her head and eased the front door open a little wider, terrified of what she might find. But the living room looked like it always did. John was passed out on the couch, snoring heavily, his body no longer twisted by the boo hag's power. Ellie and Tasha stood in the entryway and exchanged a look.

"He must've come back here after the hag rode him," Ellie whispered.

Sunlight streamed into the trailer then, and Ms. Washington emerged from her bedroom, looking more rested than she had in days. "Tasha! You're up early. How did you sleep last night?"

Her grandmother's encounters with the boo hag must have taken a toll on her, Tasha thought. Ms. Washington didn't even remember that she was supposed to have slept at Kim's. "Okay. I got up early so I could help Ellie water her tomatoes this morning."

She elbowed Ellie, who startled and stifled a yawn. "That's right! The plants are doing great, thanks to Tasha's help. How are you doing, Ms. Washington?"

Tasha's grandmother smiled warmly. "Good, thank you for asking. I got my first good night's sleep and now I am ready for some breakfast. Ellie, do you like waffles?"

"I like pancakes better," Ellie said.

Tasha nodded. "I'd like some pancakes."

Ms. Washington nodded. "Pancakes it is, then."

Kim's house burned to the ground the night she died. John went by after waking up. Like Ms. Washington, he had no memory of the previous night, and he couldn't understand why Kim wasn't answering his texts. He returned much later, with a story about having found the house a smoldering ruin. The police and fire department were there, and they told John they didn't find Kim's body—only the charred remains of some kind of animal on the patio. John continued to text and call her, but there was no response. It was like she had disappeared into the night.

As the days turned into a week with no sign of Kim, John came to accept that she had just left town. He didn't seem all that upset about it, but Tasha caught him, at times, staring out the window sadly, playing with a small scrap of fabric he must have found at her house, a charred piece of the dress with the cats and the yarn. He never talked about her, though, and soon was back to his old smiling self. Perhaps this was because whatever spell Kim had cast on him was fading. Or, maybe, it was just because he was too prideful to admit that someone, for once, had decided to leave him.

John moved back into Ms. Washington's trailer. Neither he nor Ms. Washington talked about what had happened with Kim—they seemed to decide that their fight about his sudden proposal was one they didn't need to talk about. Which was probably for the best.

After a couple weeks had passed and the cleanup crews had dispersed, Tasha and Ellie snuck over to where Kim's house had been. It was almost as though she had never lived there, and Tasha felt a momentary pang of sadness—but she quickly shook it off. Kim had been really nice, but she also skinned people. There wasn't any amount of nice that could make up for that.

Besides, as much as Tasha might have missed the time she had with the person she thought Kim was, she missed her own mom more. And if she could learn to live with that pain, then she could definitely get over the boo hag.

When school started that fall Ellie introduced Tasha to all her friends. Ellie knew everyone, and if there was anyone who tried to mess with Tasha, she took care of it. It was great. Tasha had never had such a loyal friend before, and she worked hard to be just as good a friend to Ellie. Especially since it looked like, for once, she was in a place that would be her home for a long time.

Tasha came home every day to freshly baked cookies and her grandma waiting to hear about her day. She had hoped that after the boo hag was gone, her father might decide he wanted to be around more, but that wasn't the case. He eventually found a new girlfriend, moved out and into her apartment, and was rarely around after that. Tasha couldn't pretend she wasn't hurt by it all over again. But she also knew that maybe he was never meant to be a parent, and she tried to be okay with that. Fortunately, she had an amazing grandmother, not to mention a best friend who was ready to fight monsters for her.

Some days when Tasha's grief got the best of her, or when the memories of her first few weeks at Shady Pines Estates started to feel like something that had happened to someone else, she took out the dress Kim had made her and put it on. And in those moments, she tried to remember how nice Kim had been when she wasn't skinning and eating the souls of old people. Wherever she was, Tasha hoped there were lots of fun dresses and material to sew with.

But she was mostly glad that everyone she loved still had their skin.

EPILOGUE

Elaina swallowed dryly, her heart finally returning to something like a normal rhythm. She had barely moved as the woman told her story, and Elaina was pretty sure her feet had fallen asleep from sitting in the same space for so long.

"So, that's it?" Elaina said when the silence had dragged on for too long.

"Hmm. Perhaps. Were you scared? Just absolutely terrified?" The old woman seemed to be testing Elaina, and she wasn't quite sure what to say.

She shrugged. "I dunno. I guess."

At that, the witch sighed and murmured something that sounded like "children these days" before tapping her chin. "No, I don't think you were. So, I will ask you one last question. Can you do me a favor before you go?"

"Uh, sure." Elaina stood, and as she did the door to the cabin slowly creaked open. She wasn't really sure she wanted to go back out into the night.

The witch leaned forward, a terrible expression on her face, half delight, half malice. "I want you to run."

Elaina frowned in confusion. "You want me to . . . run?"

The witch nodded. "Yessssss," she said, sitting back in her chair. "If the story didn't do the trick, I'd hate for you to be caught too quickly. Your fear will be far tastier if it has a chance to *marinate*."

Before Elaina could figure out what the old woman meant, a croaking, hissing sound came from behind her, and she turned, slowly, her heart pounding anew.

Slinking down the hall was what could only be a boo hag come to life. The creature was worse than Elaina had imagined when hearing the story—a misshapen figure, skinless, muscles exposed and covered in the thickest, reddest blood. The claws at the end of the hands were black and curved and glinted in the low light of the cabin. She didn't want to look at its face, but she did. The sunken eyes glowed, and the fierce gaze held her in place.

She wanted to run, wanted to flee, but her legs were jelly and she couldn't move no matter how hard she tried. It wasn't until the old woman cackled—the sound like the screech of an unoiled door hinge—that Elaina was able to break free of her terror and sprint out the cabin door and into the fog, the old woman shouting after her.

As Elaina darted blindly through the trees in what she hoped was the direction back to camp, the witch's parting screams echoed through Elaina's mind, driving her forward faster than she had ever run before.

"Delicious!"

ABOUT THE AUTHOR

JUSTINA IRELAND is the *New York Times* best-selling author of the critically acclaimed YA novels *Rust in the Root, Dread Nation,* and *Deathless Divide,* as well as the Scott O'Dell Award–winning novel *Ophie's Ghosts.* She is also one of the creators behind the Star Wars High Republic book series and the author of the novels *A Test of Courage, Mission to Disaster,* and *Out of the Shadows.* Justina lives with her family in Maryland; you can visit her online at justinaireland.com.